property
of
M.R.M.

How I Fell in LOVE &

Learned to
Shoot
Free Throws

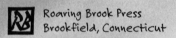 Roaring Brook Press
Brookfield, Connecticut

Jon Ripslinger

How I Fell in LOVE &

Learned to Shoot Free Throws

Published by Roaring Brook Press
A division of The Millbrook Press
2 Old New Milford Road
Brookfield, Connecticut 06804

Library of Congress Cataloging-in-Publication Data

Ripslinger, Jon.
  How I fell in love & learned to shoot free throws / by Jon
Ripslinger.
    p. cm.
  Summary: Seventeen-year-old Danny Henderson, an indif-
ferent basketball player, has his eye on Angel McPherson, star
of the girls' team in their Iowa high school.
    [1. Basketball--Fiction. 2. High schools--Fiction. 3. Schools
--Fiction.]   I. Title. II. Title: How I fell in love and learned
to shoot free throws.
  PZ7.R489Ho 2003
  [Fic]--dc21   2002013348

ISBN 0-7613-2747-9 (library binding)
10 9 8 7 6 5 4 3 2 1

ISBN 0-7613-1892-5 (trade edition)
10 9 8 7 6 5 4 3 2 1

Printed in the United States of America

For my wife, Colette, with love, and our six kids and their families. You guys keep Mom and me young.

A special thanks to Aaron King, Jennifer Ripslinger, Sharene Martin, Robert Brown, and Deborah Brodie.

1.

I'd secretly fixed an eye on Angel McPherson the moment she arrived at Big River High School, at the beginning of the girls' basketball season six months ago, and now was my chance to put a move on her.

Me, Danny Henderson, who'd never had a serious date in his life, was going to hit on the Stone Angel.

I studied her now as she stepped, relaxed and confident, to the free-throw line, bouncing the basketball, eyeing the hoop, her blond ponytail bobbing. Dressed like her, in a red-and-white Falcons basketball uniform, I crouched on my haunches on the sideline at center court in our overcrowded gym. We call our gym the Bird Cage—it's that small.

I was waiting my turn at the hoop for the free-throw shooting contest at our annual spring charity assembly. The student council sponsors the assembly in the gym during the first week of April every year. Kids pay a dollar to listen to student air bands, participate in throwing pies at volunteer teachers, and watch the principal kiss a pig. Someone always asks, "Which one is the pig?"

"The one with the wiggly tail."

"I still can't tell the difference."

We can also watch a free-throw shooting contest between a member of the boys' basketball team and a member of the girls' team. The money we raise goes to help handicapped kids.

My best friend and teammate, Tony Gomez, stood behind me for moral support.

I eyed Angel McPherson harder. She was probably the best female basketball player in the state of Iowa, an all-state center, playing on an undefeated team that had won the state championship a month ago. Awesome for a small-town high school in eastern Iowa on the banks of the Mississippi River.

We boys had stumbled to a 5–16 mark. Pretty bad.

Every girl in the gym was rooting for Angel. Their piercing screams made me wince. She was so cool in her basketball outfit, I figured ninety percent of the guys were rooting for her, too.

Angel stopped dribbling, took a deep breath.

Silence reigned in the gym.

Blowing out a long breath, she hoisted the palmed ball to eye level in her right hand, the left balancing it. She bent her knees, then lofted her shot in a high arc toward the basket with perfect rotation, her wrist and fingers extending for follow-through.

Swish! Nothing but net. Another girl from the girls' team chased the ball down and tossed it back to Angel.

"Nice form," Tony whispered in my ear. "And she can shoot the basketball."

Angel nailed her second shot, and I thought the girls' shrieks would split the gym's walls and burst the windows.

In a team meeting, Coach Dunlap had begged for someone to step up and challenge Angel. The contest was a no-win situation for a guy. If he won, he had beaten a girl. What pride could he take in that? If he lost, he faced humiliation and ridicule. Who wanted that?

Fully understanding the downside, I stepped forward, saying I didn't mind doing a good deed for charity, even if I might look foolish. I had a lot to be thankful for compared to handicapped kids, which was true, but everyone looked at me as if I were crazy. Not a single guy knew of my secret wish to sidle up to Angel.

She popped in her third, fourth, and fifth shots. All net. She was in rhythm now.

The gym rocked with even louder shrieks.

I swallowed and shifted my haunches.

Another thing. Dunlap said he was glad I had volunteered, because I needed all the practice I could get shooting free throws under pressure. He was right about that.

When she dropped in her tenth consecutive free throw, the entire student body—faculty included—stood and clapped and cheered for her.

"We're number one! We're number one!" the girls chanted, pounding their fists in the air.

I stood up on the sidelines, my throat dry. I hadn't expected to feel this shaky, but if my strategy worked, the shakes were worth it. And the humiliation of losing to her.

"Just relax, buddy," Tony said. "You can beat her. Keep telling yourself that."

The contest format was simple enough. Each shooter would take twenty-five shots. Ten for the first shooter, ten for the second, followed by another round of ten for each shooter, then a round of five.

The most baskets out of twenty-five won. Each shooter had to take twenty-five shots, even if things looked hopeless for him or her near the end.

Angel turned and flicked me the ball, a chest-high shot with steam behind it, her face expressionless, her eyes sliding away from mine.

As I dribbled the ball to the free-throw line, I paused a moment when she passed me, and made my first move on her, saying, "Nice shooting."

She looked at me again. Blankly. Maybe surprised. "Thanks."

For the first time, I noticed that her mouth was tilted a little, not much, as if someone had pasted it onto her face crooked.

She'd worked up a nice sweat. Beads of perspiration sprinkled her forehead and clung to her full upper lip. She'd probably been loosening up in the upper gym before the contest started. I should've thought of that.

As I stood at the free-throw circle, bouncing the ball with my right hand, then my left, my knees felt weak, my palms, damp. Just like first-game jitters.

Tony stood under the basket, ready to retrieve the ball. "C'mon, buddy. Just do it. Beat her."

I sucked in a deep breath.

I'd shot fifty-eight percent for the season. I'm sure Angel shot higher than that. I'd lost the boys' opening game of the season last November, 55–54, when I'd failed to convert two free throws with three seconds left in an overtime period.

What I wanted to do now was look good, but not too good, while losing to her.

I stopped dribbling. I tuned out the noise from the crowd.

With my eyes fixed on the rim, no hesitation, I poked my first shot at the basket, a jerky movement. The ball hit the front of the hoop, bounced up, over, and in. A sloppy shot at best. But a basket.

"Relax, buddy," Tony said, tossing the ball back. "Just relax."

I sucked in another breath, blew it out, but my second

shot wasn't much better, clanking off the back of the rim this time, bounding high, then diving through the net. And so it was with each one of my shots, shaky attempts that hit, bounced off of, or spun around the rim before wobbling into the net. Never a clean shot.

I lost track of how many attempts I had made, but I knew I'd missed only one, and I couldn't believe it when Tony bounced the ball to me and said, "That's nine out of ten. You did good."

I felt a bit relaxed now, knowing my plan was working perfectly.

As Angel trotted across the floor toward me, I handed her the ball and said, "Your turn."

She paused. "Awesome shooting." She said it with a smile. Definitely, her mouth had a tiny tilt. I'd always thought blonds with blue eyes were a cliché. Angel's eyes were gray.

"I got lucky," I said, and wished I hadn't admitted that.

Pressure didn't mean anything to her. That's why everyone called her Stone Angel. "This newcomer from Florida plays the game with cool, efficient athleticism." That's a quote from the *Big River Times*.

Now, her fans backing her with wild cheers, she rippled the net nine straight times with picture-perfect shots. Even her last shot in the second set should have fallen, but it spun around inside the rim, looked as if it would drop through, but popped out. Shots like that had dropped for me.

She shook her head and bit her bottom lip. She was disappointed. She'd expected to hit twenty-five straight. She might just as well have.

I fell apart in the second round, canning only five of ten shots. Rim shots that had dropped for me in the first round refused to fall this time, and with each miss, my mouth turned a bit dryer, my palms a bit sweatier.

Male boos from the crowd rang in my ears, and it was their voices that yelled, "Ain't we got anybody better?"

"What's wrong with you?" Tony patted me on the butt and walked off the court with me. "You're letting that stupid girl get to you. The crowd, too." He pivoted and snapped the ball to Angel.

My face felt hot. "Too late now. What's the count?"

"Nineteen, fourteen. She might blow a couple of these."

"I doubt it."

Angel missed her first attempt in the final five. But she steadied herself, appeared to concentrate a little harder, took more time between shots, and nailed the next four.

The girls went wild with cheers.

Not feeling any pressure now, I stepped to the line, dribbled the ball, and drilled four of my next five shots, my best-looking attempts all day. Finished, wiping my palms on my shorts, I gave a sigh of relief. I'd lost 23–18, but had surprised myself with my showing. Just what I wanted: I hadn't looked totally stupid. Still, I was a free-throw shooter in need of help.

Everyone in the bleachers stood and applauded. Shrieks and whistles riddled the gym. Angel stood motionless, arms at her sides, smiling a little but looking embarrassed, and gave a tiny wave of acknowledgment to the crowd.

"And the winnerrrr issssss," Dr. Johnson, the principal, bawled in deep tones over the gym PA system, as if he were announcing the champion in a heavyweight world-title boxing match, "Angelll McPherrrsonnn!"

The chant "Angel! Angel! Angel!" roared through the gym.

Tony smiled and whacked me on the back. "You did

okay, buddy. You want to know the truth, I didn't think you'd do that good."

"Thanks."

I drifted over to where Angel stood on the sideline, Tony right behind me. Time to put the main part of my game plan into action.

"You were great," I said.

"Too bad someone had to lose."

Her hand snapped out. I stared at it a moment like a dummy, as if I didn't know what to do, my hands dangling at the end of my arms.

"You had one little bad streak," she said, and was about to withdraw her hand, but I reached out at the last second, clutched it, and pumped twice, feeling the imprint of her sweaty flesh on mine.

"You're the champ," I said.

"Doesn't make any difference. We're all here for charity, not honors."

I'm six-five, two-thirty, and Angel is maybe a head shorter than I am, five-ten, one-thirty. She's no Barbie doll. A couple of skinny running backs on our football team would kill to have her thighs.

I took a breath. "I wish you'd teach me how to shoot free throws," I said, the words popping out of my mouth, just as I'd rehearsed them.

I spotted Tony's frown.

"Are you serious?" she said.

"I shot fifty-eight percent last season. Not even close to what you probably shot."

"You shot well today."

"Luck."

"He's not as bad as he thinks he is," Tony said.

I swallowed. "Maybe sometime, um, we could get together, you know, and shoot some."

She looked at me. Her eyes were pure gray.

I knew she was trying to figure out if I was serious or not.

Just as she started to answer me, Mr. Voss, a driver's ed teacher, marched up to us and said, "You guys are going to have to move now. We have to set up for the next presentation. Nice goin', Angel." He didn't say a thing to me.

Then Angel turned, and right before my eyes, before I could get an answer, she flew away.

"Cool move," Tony said, "asking the Stone Angel to teach you how to shoot free throws. Never thought you had it in you, buddy."

Tony and I had escaped to the boys' locker room.

I hung up my shorts and jersey in my locker on a hanger, and slipped my jeans off the locker's back hook. The sweaty-smelling locker room was empty except for the two of us, and our voices sounded loud and hollow, as if we were in a cavern.

Teachers who had volunteered were being auctioned off now as student servants for a day. No kid in the building wanted to miss the bidding and the sight of a teacher servant carrying a kid's books or hauling a kid's backpack around, all stooped over.

Me, I didn't want to go back to the gym. After losing, I didn't want to face anyone. Especially my dad. He's a PE teacher, head football coach, and head of the athletic department at West. He wouldn't say anything to me, not in front of everybody, anyway, but I still didn't want to face him.

I could just hear some of the other guys on the basketball team, though. "You lost to a girl! What a maggot!"

Tony said with a grin, "Having her teach you to shoot free throws is not really what's on your mind, is it, buddy?"

Jeans on, I slipped my T-shirt over the top of my head.

"You're missing the assembly. I can dress myself," I said with a smirk.

"If you're finally going to hit on a girl, you've picked the wrong one. She's weird."

"All I asked her to do was teach me to shoot free throws." I sat on the bench. Pulled on my socks. "I'm surprised I even said that."

"Give me a break. Dunlap's been trying to teach you to shoot free throws for the past two seasons. And so have I. You don't remember the half hour we spent each night after practice this year?"

It's true. Tony had tried to help me. He's a guard on our team, so quick and crafty we call him the Fox. Last season he averaged 8.9 assists a game, most of them to me, the Bruiser with power underneath. He's an over-eighty-percent free-throw shooter, too, a natural talent with his own quirky way of shooting. When he tries to help me, he says, "Just watch me, then do it." But I can't.

We'll both be back next year, the only varsity seniors.

"This girl's got a technique," I said. "She could show me."

Tony gave me a big smile. He has the whitest teeth. "Melody knows a few girls with good technique, too. She'd love to fix you up again."

"Another Amber Clarke? No thanks."

"That was your fault."

"Right."

"Someone really hot."

"Free throws, that's all I'm interested in."

"Whatever. Let's go back to the gym."

2.

My dad and I live alone. Always have since I can remember.

Dad likes to cook. Not fancy stuff. Chops, steaks, ribs. Mostly on the grill. All winter, even in the worst snowstorms, he grills outside on charcoal. No gas grill for Dad. He even has a hog cooker in the backyard on wheels. A boat, too. Seventeen-foot Crestliner.

At suppertime, I set the table, get a salad ready and a vegetable. We both clean up the kitchen after and stack the dishwasher. About once a week, we fire it up.

That night after the charity assembly, Dad was outside cooking chicken breasts. It was a warm April night with a blue sky turning quickly to dusk, the ground soaked from a week of rain, the grass turning green.

I was thinking this was going to be a typical school night for Dad and me. Supper and a discussion of my day. Homework, a little TV, maybe a telephone talk with Tony. Lights out by eleven. All very predictable.

Except that tonight, I was wondering what to do about Angel. Nearly everything had gone right for me at the assembly. I'd lost the free-throw contest, but had made a respectable showing. Sort of. Anyone who knew anything about basketball could tell I needed help at the line. I'd asked Angel for lessons but hadn't gotten an answer.

What now? Call her? I didn't know her telephone number or where she lived. Didn't know her dad's first name. The telephone book listed fifteen McPhersons. Pretty big job to call all of them, asking for Angel. But not impossible.

Dad brought in four golden brown chicken breasts on a wooden platter. I set our bowls of tossed salad into place on the table and retrieved the baked potatoes from the microwave, dropping one onto each plate.

"Got everything?" Dad said, settling his bulky frame into his chair.

"Think so. Chicken looks good."

"Salad, too, Chief."

Dad calls me Chief. I don't know why, since I'm definitely not the Chief around here. I take all the orders. Give none.

I sat down. We said a blessing and dug in.

You'd think my dad and I had a perfect life together, like two bachelors who got along perfectly. Or two brothers who shared everything, me the younger one, obviously, and Dad the older one who provided everything for his little brother: golf clubs, shotgun, rifle, bow and arrows, rods and reels, pool table, skis. Jeep. And the big brother spent time with the little brother, teaching the little brother how to use all this expensive sporting gear proficiently.

"Don't let that free-throw thing bother you," Dad said, and reached across the table for the margarine. The plastic tub disappeared in his paw. "Basketball's not your thing anyway."

"Nobody wanted to do it," I said. "Dunlap said I could use the practice under pressure."

"It's supposed to be a fun thing." Dad swabbed more margarine on his potatoes and corn. He's big, six-five, two-ninety now, a former Michigan State University all-America tackle. A bad knee kept him out of the pros. "The kids take it too seriously. Especially the females."

He never calls them women or girls. Always females.

"I'm surprised I made eighteen." I chewed a bite of

chicken. Vacuumed in some salad. I'm hungry most of the time. I even like the cafeteria food at school, and I'm lucky Dad's a decent cook.

"Don't worry about losing," Dad said. "Keep your head on straight. This spring we'll do a little fishing, golfing, then you can help me out at summer football camp, and soon fall will be here, and football your senior year."

That wasn't the way I pictured my next couple of months. I pictured myself working during the day, earning my own money for the first time in my life, and wallowing in the clutches of Angel McPherson at night.

The phone rang. Dad set his can of beer down. He always has one with supper. Old Style Lite. Still at the table, he reached with a long arm for the phone on the wall.

"Hendersons," he said, and lifted the coiled phone cord out of his way so it wouldn't fall into his plate. His head didn't move, but his eyes shifted toward me.

"Angel McPherson wants to talk to you," he said.

My mouth dropped open and froze there a second.

"Who?"

"That free-throw-shooting female from the contest." Dad thrust the phone at me.

I didn't move.

"If you don't want to talk to her—"

"I do!" I grabbed the phone from him, cleared my throat. "H-hello . . ." The word stumbled out of my mouth.

"Hi." Her voice was soft, almost a whisper. "I'm sorry, is this a bad time?"

"I'm eating, but it's not a bad time." I glanced at Dad. He was stabbing a chunk of lettuce, along with a slice of carrot and radish, all smeared with blue-cheese dressing. "What's up?" I tried to sound nonchalant.

"Maybe I should call back later."

"No . . . no, this is all right." I glanced at Dad. "I'll tell you what, hang on just a second."

I stood up and hiked the coiled cord over Dad's head, setting the receiver on the other side of the table. "Hang this up in a second, will you?"

"What's she want?"

I shrugged. "She wants to talk to me."

I bolted from the kitchen before Dad could ask another question. Grabbed the cordless from off the TV in the living room. Down the hallway I ran. In my room, I closed the door and flopped onto my bed on my back, phone jammed to my ear.

"Still there?"

"Oh, hi," Angel said, and I suddenly thought a real angel's voice would be just as soft as hers.

"Dad?" I said. "Hang up." I waited a second. "Dad!"

Click!

"Hi," I said.

"Hi," she repeated. "I . . . didn't know if I should call or not." She sounded nervous. "Are you serious about learning to shoot free throws?"

"Sure."

She didn't say anything else for a second.

"Are you offering to give me lessons?" I said.

"Sort of. I mean, yes, if you wouldn't mind."

"Why would I mind? I asked you."

"Because you're a guy. I don't think there's a guy athlete in the world who thinks, down deep, he can learn something from a girl." She sounded a little defensive.

"Unless he just got beaten by one," I said.

"I'm offering because I could use some help myself on the boards. Rebounding. Blocking out. There's nobody big enough on the girls' team to practice against."

"Hammering people underneath," I said, "that's my

specialty. Sometimes guys on the team call me the Bruiser."

"I play like a girl underneath the basket, I'm not afraid to admit it. I get pushed around, beat on, intimidated."

I said, "What you're saying is, we can work out together, so we can improve each other's game? Is that it?"

Another brief silence. "I knew you wouldn't like the idea."

"I didn't say that."

"I don't know why I humiliated myself this way. Good-bye."

"Hey, wait! Wait! Don't hang up! It's a great idea."

"Don't lie to me."

"I'm not. I am interested, I am. Honest. I was thinking about calling you myself."

"Another lie."

"Really. Except—"

Click! She hung up. Just like that. I blinked. The dial tone buzzed in my ear. I stared at the phone. What had I done wrong? Why had she changed her mind so fast? I sat on the edge of my bed, trying to figure it out. Maybe she never expected me to say yes to my helping her, and when I did, she chickened out. That's it.

But then why call?

Back to supper.

When I slid onto my chair at the kitchen table, Dad said, "What was that all about?"

He never takes "nothing" for an answer, so I either have to tell him the truth or tell him little white lies. Generally, I tell the truth, but I don't feel too guilty about the white lies. He had told me monumental lies about my mom.

"She wanted to play basketball."

Dad looked at me with a frown. "Basketball? That female? But why?"

I puffed my cheeks. "She said she'd help me with free throws, and she wanted me to help her with moves underneath." I shrugged. "Stupid, huh?"

I could almost hear Dad's mind churning inside his skull as he finished his last bite of chicken.

"Not a good plan, Chief," he said. "First thing you know, you'd hurt her, then we'd get sued. Besides, females and males weren't meant to compete against each other in sports." He set his fork down, wiped his lips with a napkin. "What did you tell her?"

I poked my chicken around my plate with my fork. "I think she got ticked off at me. She hung up. She must've decided it was a bad idea, too."

"Just as well," Dad said.

That night as I lay in bed, twisted up in my covers, trying to fall asleep, I could still hear Angel's whispery voice in my ear. Somehow I'd dropped the ball. I'd given her the impression I didn't like her idea, maybe didn't like her. But I did.

I rolled over in bed. Tugged the blanket over me. Punched the pillow. Heard a dog bark outside. Punched the pillow again.

I'd gotten this far with Angel, I couldn't stop now.

3.

"I can't believe she called," Tony said.

We were sitting in the cab of his red Ranger Ford pickup on a bright sunny morning in the school parking lot, watching kids straggle into school. Time: 7:30 A.M. We had five minutes before we needed to make our dash. Classes start at 7:45.

Using a clipboard to write on, Tony always does his last-minute homework in the morning in his truck. He says it's the only quiet place he can find because he has five younger brothers and sisters at home who never keep their mouths shut. If he goes into the school building, he always gets sidetracked.

"She called all right"—I'd already told him everything— "and today I'm going to track her down."

"I talked to Melody," Tony said. "We both think you can do better."

"She's the coolest girl in school. Maybe the universe, as far as I'm concerned."

"She brushes guys off like flies. No close girlfriends, either. She's always alone. Even her teammates don't know her very well."

"She's a loner, so what? But didn't you hear the way everyone cheered for her in the assembly? Somebody must like her."

"Mostly bloodthirsty girls who wanted to see her beat your sorry ass, not her friends. She has none. How you going to find her?" he said. "Over seventeen hundred kids in this school."

"Hang out by her locker. I know where it is. I remember seeing it decorated when the girls went to state."

"Whatever." Tony glanced at the dash clock. He gathered his books, shoved the clipboard under his seat, and dug for the door handle. "I think you're making a mistake, buddy. I can't believe she called you," he said again.

As Tony and I galloped into the school building and I rooted in my locker for my books, I felt a little pissed that Tony should be surprised that Angel called me.

In junior high, girls called me on the phone at night a lot, but Dad answered most of the time and put an end to that. "He's doing his homework," I'd hear him growl.

"Don't bother him. Don't you have something better to do?" Everyone knew he was the high school football coach and had a reputation for being a bear.

Sometimes I answered the phone, but that was even worse. I'd stumble around, not knowing what to say, especially because Dad never left the room, and the conversations always fizzled after two or three minutes. By the time I got to high school, the word was out that I had a mean old man. I was good at football, okay at basketball, but socially a dork. Don't bother with Danny Henderson. Waste of time. So mostly I just hung with guys and tried to blend in.

Still, I'd gained a little experience. I went to a drive-in movie last summer with Melody and Tony. The only drive-in left in Iowa is near here by Maquoketa. Melody had fixed me up with Amber Clarke, a little brunette, so tiny she felt like a doll in my arms. We gobbled lips in the back seat of Tony's dad's Buick Century. Lots of room. Practically had her blouse off. She had breasts the size of cupcakes. I pictured them topped with frosting and a cherry, though I was too chicken that night to find out.

I took her swimming at the city pool and to a rock concert. I talked to her on the phone a lot from Tony's house. I liked her, and I thought she liked me. I thought things were going pretty well, but I always hesitated to put any serious moves on her. I just couldn't do it. My hands felt like stones, and I kept wondering what Dad would say. "Next time," I'd tell myself. And Tony.

Then, near the end of summer, she suddenly didn't have time for me anymore. One night over the phone, she said, "Don't call me, Danny." Melody said she'd fallen for a guy from a different school. "You were too slow, Danny," Melody said. "Losing her was your own fault." Last fall when school started, whenever Amber and I passed each other in the halls, she ignored me. How lame is that?

Angel McPherson's locker is right next to the library, second floor. It was way out of my way, but I figured I'd reroute myself so I could pass it. The first time I spotted her, I'd stroll right by and simply nod hello. See if she smiled or frowned at me. Then I'd return a period or two later and maybe walk with her to her next class. Break the ice again.

The detour made me late for Spanish II, first floor, third period, opposite end of the building, and earned me a detention. Worse, Angel was never at her locker. Didn't she use it?

Maybe she had a boyfriend now and shared his locker.

At noon, Dad caught me in the hall, just as I rounded the corner by the office, heading to the cafeteria for lunch, ahead of the pack. The bad part of having your dad on the faculty is you can't get away from him.

Dad said, "You want to hit some golf balls after school with Brian and me?" Brian Castle is Dad's defensive back coach, a small but compact, well-built guy who can hit a golf ball farther than Dad or I can.

"Um, I don't think so. I got something else to do."

"What? You need to work on that slice of yours, Chief. You need more work with that new putter, too."

"I might mess around in the park this afternoon."

Dad frowned. "Basketball with that female?"

"I haven't even seen her today."

Dad shook his head. Before he could say anything else, I plunged into the horde of students stampeding for lunch.

I decided to give Angel's locker one more shot after school. It was late when I got there because Mr. Herrick made me stay after class to get help in chemistry. Most kids had already cleared out of the halls, and as I came zipping around the corner by the library, I stopped in my tracks.

There she was, Angel McPherson, dressed in jeans and a sweatshirt, blond hair loose, falling across her shoulders, head down as she spun the dial on her combination lock. Her backpack and a stack of books squatted on the floor by her feet.

I straightened myself. Took a deep breath. Exhaled. Swallowed. Approached cautiously, almost on tiptoe.

This time I hadn't rehearsed exactly what I wanted to say, and what came out was, "Need help?"

She gave a start and jerked around to face me. She blinked.

"Hi," I said. "Need help with that?" I tried to smile, but felt I was grinning inanely.

"Hello," she said, almost shyly, tucking her hair behind her ears.

She probably still didn't know all the little survival tactics a person needed to know in this school. I said, "Sometimes those things open if you let the lock hang down, rather than hold it up in your palm when you dial the numbers."

"For real?"

"Honest."

"Damn thing hasn't worked right all year."

Angel let the lock hang from the locker latch, spun the dial, and slowly picked out the three-digit combination. Bingo! She pulled it open with a click.

She turned to me with a dazzling smile. When she

smiled like that, you couldn't tell her mouth was tilted at all. "Thanks," she said.

"It's an old trick."

She picked her books off the floor and stacked them neatly on the bottom shelf. "What are you doing here? I haven't seen you in this part of the building before." She pulled out a couple of notebooks, unzipped her pack, and stuffed them in.

"Lost." I hoped I sounded clever, but when she didn't smile, I quickly added, "Actually, I was going to do some research in the library." I glanced at the wall clock halfway down the hall. "But it's almost three, time for the library to close."

"It closes at four. I've got to run, someone's waiting for me. Thanks."

Panic. "Can—may I walk with you?"

"What about your research?"

"It can wait."

I picked up her pack—it weighed a ton—and was going to carry it for her, but she snatched the strap out of my hand and said, "You don't have to do that."

I fell in step beside her. We marched along in silence for a moment, sidestepping the custodian, Mr. Robertson, pushing a wide dust mop back and forth the whole length of the hallway. We all said hello.

Then, after we passed him, Angel and I spoke at the same time. "About last night—"

We laughed.

"I'm sorry I bothered you last night," she said before I could get started again.

"I'm glad you called."

"It was a stupid thing to do. Every once in a while, I act on impulse and hate myself for it later."

"I like your idea."

We hung a left, then a sharp right, and scuffed down the stairs. She said, "I could tell by the way you kept hesitating I'd made a mistake."

"I wasn't hesitating."

"Yes, you were."

At the foot of the stairs, I touched her shoulder, halting her. She backed up against the cinder-block wall, her backpack scraping.

"Look," I said, listening to the words rumbling through my head before I spoke. "You and me—I—playing basketball, working on our game, I think it's a great idea. We could start right away. Like this afternoon. Four o'clock."

"You're not serious."

I rolled my eyes. "I am. Why do you think I came strolling up to your locker just minutes ago? I mean, I've passed your locker between every class today, looking for you."

"Have you?"

"I swear."

"I wasn't in school today. I came by to pick up some things I need."

"The proper free-throw shooting technique, that's what I really want to research." Almost the truth.

She smiled. "You're not kidding, are you?"

Were girls always so doubtful? "Nope."

The rest wasn't too bad. We decided the school's basketball court outside was not a good place to work out. It was always too crowded. Same for the school gym. I was especially glad we didn't decide on the school courts, because I didn't want my dad or the rest of the guys at school to know I was playing basketball against a girl, trying to learn something. Long ago, Dad had constructed a basket for me above our two-car garage, but I didn't mention that. We decided on using the hoops at Duck Creek Park in about an hour.

"You want me to pick you up?" I said.

"I live by the creek. The bike path that runs along the creek goes by my backyard, right to the park. I'll walk or ride a bike."

"Deal," I said, and offered my hand.

"Deal."

We shook, pumping once, the second time I'd shaken hands with her.

Angel glimpsed the wall clock. "Oh, wow! I've got to run." We raced down the hall and around the corner to the school's front entrance.

"That's my ride." Angel pointed to a shiny red Grand Am, parked in the fire lane, motor running.

"I'll walk out to the car with you."

I pushed the wide glass door open, and Angel rested a hand on my forearm. "No. Please."

I looked at her, her mouth a little tight around the edges.

"Please," she repeated.

"All right. See you in a bit."

I held the door for her, and she sprinted out the door toward the car, blond hair flying. Shrugging out of her pack, she slid into the seat, the driver wheeling away before Angel hardly had a chance to pull the door closed.

I puffed out a long breath.

Big event for me.

What would Dad think, my hustling a girl on my own this time? He didn't need to know. I hadn't told him about Amber Clarke. It wasn't like he'd never kept a secret from me. And because of him, I had made a fool of myself, writing letters to my dead mom.

4.

The first letter I wrote to my mom was an English assignment, like back in fourth grade. I should've kept it. It was my best one. The assignment was to write to somebody famous from history that you admired and wished you'd been friends with. Benjamin Franklin, maybe. Or Jackie Robinson. One girl wrote to the Statue of Liberty. She got an A.

I wrote to my mom.

At the time, I thought she'd died of cancer and was in heaven. I told her, even though I'd never known her, I missed her. I knew from the few pictures I had of her that she was young, with a round face, a big smile, and dark brown eyes. But I wanted to hear her breathe and laugh. How about the touch of her fingertips? What kind of perfume did she like? What did she think of me? Was I an okay kid? Or did I cry all the time? Did she really like me? Was she good at math and English? I am. But not science or history. How did she and Dad meet? He won't talk to me about that stuff. Not a word.

Part of the assignment was to read the letter aloud in a quiet place, like your room, or outside, say in a park or the woods. Ms. Shannon, our teacher, said that would allow you to communicate as closely as possible with that person.

On a bright sunny day in April, blue skies, cardinals singing, I read my letter to my mom in the cemetery, over her gravestone: NICOLE HOWARD-HENDERSON. BELOVED DAUGHTER. No mention of WIFE or MOTHER.

By the time I finished, I felt choked, an ache in my throat. I felt my mom's presence for sure, as if she were alive in the touch of the warm sunshine. I felt her in the breeze, and I felt sad because I knew she'd never be able to write back.

My heart dropped when Ms. Shannon returned my letter with a C– on it. "A very touching letter, Daniel," she said. "But your mother is not a famous historical person."

"But she's the most important dead person in my life."

Ms. Shannon peered at me through her glasses, which had slipped down her long nose. "You must learn to follow directions, young man."

I threw the letter away.

I wrote a second time, though, two years later, when I found out the truth about my mom. A brief, bitter letter that I read over her grave one chilly, drizzly day in March, dirty-looking clouds in the sky. I called her a whore and demanded to know why she had cheated on Dad and me. What was wrong with us? Weren't we good enough for her? I told her I was mad at her and mad at Dad, too, for lying to me all this time. I'd made a fool of myself in my first letter, thinking she was such a great person. I told her I understood why Dad didn't like women, and I didn't blame him. Now I didn't like them, either. She'd never hear from me again. *Slut!* I tore the letter to shreds and burned it on her tombstone, the smell of the burning match and paper clinging to the inside of my nostrils as I trudged home.

But I wrote one more time. A letter of apology. Just last year. It took me that long to realize that girls are okay people, if a little quirky, and my dad's not always right about everything. I understood what Dad was trying to do, protecting me with a lie. And some of what happened to their marriage might have been partly his fault. I wasn't taking either person's side.

I wanted her to know I wasn't mad at her anymore, but I wouldn't be writing again. I was old enough to realize you can't really talk to dead people, but I was writing this one last time. Just in case. I burned that letter, too, on her tombstone, a crow perched on a nearby rock watching me.

5.

At four o'clock, I wheeled my red Jeep Sahara into the parking lot at Duck Creek Park, jumped out, and immediately spotted Angel at the basketball hoops.

Thirty yards away from the hoops, I halted under an oak tree, leaned against it, folded my arms, and watched as she nailed her jump shot again and again from all angles on the concrete pad. In tight, out far, baseline, top of the key. Amazing.

She'd explode with a hard dribble, left or right hand, suddenly stop, then the crouch, the leap, and the right-handed release, this time from the baseline, the ball splitting the net. She wore cutoff jeans and a baggy, sleeveless white sweatshirt. Too bad about it being baggy. You could see the muscles rippling her long legs, though.

One of her shots hit the rim, skipped away, and when she tracked it down, she looked up and spied me leaning against the oak.

She flashed a smile. "Hi, Danny! How long you been standing there?" Her hair was slicked back into a ponytail.

I was trying to be cool leaning against the tree, ankles crossed, arms folded, head tilted. But the moment she spoke my name—the first time—I felt my face warming up.

"Been standing here an hour," I said, and sauntered over to her.

"Don't lie." She started bouncing the basketball. Right hand, left hand. "Ready for lessons?" She'd broken into a sweat, and the wet hair around her forehead had turned dark.

"Am I first?" I asked.

She nodded and bounced the ball to me. "Show me your stuff."

At the free-throw line, I bounced the ball off the concrete four or five times, inhaled, exhaled, eyed the hoop, and launched a brick that hit the back of the rim, shot straight up, and plunged through the hoop, rattling the chain net. Just like a few shots I'd made at the charity assembly.

"How's that?"

She chased the ball down for me.

"Impressive," she said. "Try again. Keep your elbow under the ball, not out to the side. Roll the ball off the tips of your fingers." I'd been told that before. Then she said, "Keep your arm and fingers extended for half a second after you shoot, as if you were posing for a picture."

I'd heard that, too.

"Helps make sure you're following through," she said.

I tried. On my next two shots, I hit the sides of the rim—left, right—and the ball skidded and bounced away in either direction.

"Keep your elbow under the ball," Angel barked. "You're pushing the ball. Cock your wrist in front of your forehead."

"Right!"

On my next shot, I smacked the backboard and the

ball dropped through. Two more misses, then a front-of-the-rim shot tumbled up, over, and in. After that, I banged another off the rim, but way too short this time, and the ball shot back to me. Another miss.

I shook my head, realizing how lucky I'd been to make eighteen shots at the assembly.

Angel held up a hand, a signal for me to back off. "Let me see the ball."

I flipped it to her, and she stepped to the line. "Look, you have to relax, get loose." She rotated her shoulders, crouched a little, flexed her knees, wiggled her butt. "You stand there all rigid, like a mannequin. Bend a little at the knees. Don't be so jerky. Think smooth."

Then she took her time and swished five in a row, her rhythm and smoothness making the shot look so effortless I shook my head again.

"Man, I'll never be able to do that. I'm not limber enough. Or something."

"Never think negative thoughts. Only positive. Someone must've told you that."

"My dad and Dunlap a million times."

She flicked the ball to me. "I'll tell you a little secret. Visualize the ball going through the hoop."

"Say that again."

"Just before you shoot, take a deep breath, let it out, and relax."

"I do that."

"Not slowly enough, though. Take your time, then concentrate on the rim and visualize the ball leaving your hand, arcing up and in. See it go through. It takes a second."

"A pretend shot?"

"Or a ghost shot. Call it what you want, it works."

"I'll try."

"Follow your ghost shot with a real shot." She paused. "Promise you won't laugh at this."

"What?"

"More advice about your follow-through. Promise you won't laugh."

"I won't laugh."

"This is my best-kept secret. On the follow-through, I visualize reaching into a bird's nest in a tree for an egg. Like putting your hand over the rim into the basket."

I didn't laugh, but I smiled a little.

I worked on my shot twenty-five, thirty minutes, taking thirty, forty, fifty pokes at the basket, I don't know. Angel tracked the ball down, every time, and snapped it back to me. She kept yelling words of encouragement like, "That's it, that was smooth!" Then, "Nice rotation on the ball." And words of criticism: "Keep your elbow in, you're not trying to fly." Or, "Relax! You're shooting like a muscle-bound football player."

That one made my ears burn.

The hardest part was trying to visualize the ball going through the hoop before every shot. But seeing the shot made me slow down and concentrate, which is maybe what I needed to do because I was used to firing away.

"One more piece of advice," Angel said. "Concentrate on the rim before, during, and after the shot, and do not lift your head to watch the ball."

I tried another ten, fifteen shots.

Finally, I held the ball and said, "How long you been playing basketball?"

"Since junior high."

I walked over to her. "In Florida?"

She looked at me, head cocked. "St. Petersburg. How do you know where I come from?"

"I need a rest," I said. "Let's sit under a tree, the sun's hot."

"Forty-five minutes of work is not going to make you a shooter."

"I must've shot a million free throws this year; I'm still not a shooter."

"You've got to establish a routine that you follow on every attempt, a consistent technique. Anyone ever tell you that?"

"All the time."

We ambled off and sat in the grass under the oak tree, the bark scratchy against my back, the grass prickly on my stretched-out legs. Angel pulled her legs up to her chest and wrapped her arms around them, chin on her knees. The basketball lay beside me on the ground.

I said, "I read an article about you in the paper when you made all-state this year. The writer thought you were awesome. Your dad teach you to play?"

A moment's silence. "I don't have a dad."

"Oh." I hope I hadn't sounded startled. "I just assumed . . ."

"Girls can be athletes without male role models," she said, defensive.

"That's true," I said. "I didn't mean anything. . . ." My voice trailed into silence. A crow cawed in a far-off tree.

"He died in a helicopter crash," she said, as if reciting. "He was in the Air Force. A pilot."

"Combat?" I cringed a little. I shouldn't be prying. She probably didn't want to talk about it. I pictured a helicopter exploding in the air, crashing in the jungle, burning, clouds of billowing black smoke rising. "Look, I'm sorry, I didn't mean to ask that."

"He died on a training exercise in Georgia." She lifted her narrow chin. "I'm sure if he'd been in a war, he would've been a hero."

"Right."

She peered across the grassy park and stretched her legs out next to mine, not touching, but close enough to touch if I moved—I didn't—and laced her hands behind her head, against the oak. Her legs were silky smooth and curved, mine, knotty and hairy.

She looked at me and said, "Your turn, tell me about you."

I bit my bottom lip. What to say? "Everyone at school knows my dad." I cleared my throat. "You know what? You and I, we're kind of the same but different."

"How's that?"

"I don't have a mom." Then I told her The Lie that Dad had told me as a kid until the day I forced the truth out of him. I told everyone The Lie, even Tony, because the truth was too ugly and embarrassing. I had The Lie well rehearsed. "My mom died of cancer," I said. "Right after I was born. Like less than a year. She was in the hospital a long while, and she suffered a lot."

"That's terrible."

"She wrote me a letter before she died, telling me how much she loved me and how she'd miss me. Heaven would not be complete without me in her arms, she'd save a place for me, but I should take all the time in the world getting there." That part of The Lie I'd made up myself.

A sad look from Angel. "I guess we are alike, but also different." She picked at the grass. "I can't imagine not having a mom."

My head dropped. After I finished The Lie, I always felt guilty, ashamed, embarrassed—pick one—because I hadn't been up front with the person I was talking to.

I finally said, "I can't imagine not having a dad, but I wish I had a mom, too. Just to see what she would be like. Hear her voice."

"Me, too, I wish I had a dad."

Suddenly I didn't like this conversation. "C'mon. Your turn, show me your stuff."

I offered her my right hand. She took it, and I pulled her up. I loved touching her hand, a strong hand with long slender fingers.

We decided to go one-on-one. That way, we could rebound our missed shots, if she ever missed, and I could see how she worked underneath.

I tossed her the ball so she could take it out first. "Let's go," I said.

She came dribbling at me low and crouching, springing on the balls of her feet. She faked right, left, hoping to drive around me, but I slid with her fakes and watched her eyes, thinking they'd telegraph her final direction.

Fifteen feet from the basket, her back to me, my arms and body spread over her like a net, she gave me a head-fake to the right, then stepped out to her left, pivoted, and unleashed the basketball in a smooth, arching, fade-away jump shot high over my outstretched hand.

I spun, facing the basket, blocking her out, bumped her good with my butt, ready to crash the board—all wasted effort. Her shot swished through.

She'd burned me good. Finessed me out of my jock-strap. My face felt a little red.

"Beautiful shot!" I said.

"I got lucky." Big, big flashing grin.

The ball had rolled into the grass. I picked it up and dribbled in bounds at the center circle. I came straight at her, dribbling cautiously, not underestimating her, waiting to see what her defensive tactics might be.

I'm not a guard, not a ball handler. That's Tony's job. Dribbling's not my thing. I'm a rebounder, a put-back guy, a junkman. My shots are layups or jumpers six to eight feet from the hoop, so I felt strange out there alone, dribbling the ball.

She waited for me at quarter court, crouched, feet spread for balance, arms out, fingers stretched. She didn't move up to challenge me, but backed off, not at all aggressive on defense.

I decided to blow by her for an easy layup, and give her an elbow on the way if I had to, but damn if I didn't make my move and bounce the ball off my foot. She snared the loose ball, quick as a cat, and canned a baseline jumper before I knew what happened.

"Nice," I said. "Very nice." But under my breath, through gritted teeth, I muttered, "Just *wait!*"

We battled for thirty minutes, working up a great sweat in the sunshine, both of us gasping for all the oxygen our lungs could handle. She beat me at the perimeter every time, blitzing me with her arsenal of long-distance shots that either rippled the net or kissed off the backboard, diving through. I tried a few bombs, and a couple hung on the rim, then fell in. Nothing spectacular like Angel's wicked shots.

But she lacked the killer instinct on defense, and after she shot, she didn't block out or scrap for position. She never did grab a rebound, unless it was one that bounded off the rim right back at her. She didn't seem to realize seventy percent of missed shots are rebounded on the weak side.

Underneath, with my wider, taller body, longer arms, and better-timed jump, I outplayed her. She was no match for me. But what did I expect with a weight, height, and strength advantage? I'm sure she out-scored me, though

we didn't keep track, and I admired her gutsy perform-
ance.

After she tired of my bumping, shoving, and hacking,
she started giving me the same treatment, while clawing at
the ball on defense. She cussed a lot.

Finally I gasped, "How about a breather? Then I'll
show you some techniques for better rebounding."

She stood in front of me, smelling of lightly scented
sweat. I could feel the heat rising off her in waves.

"One last shot, okay?" Her face was flushed, and
strands of hair had pulled out of her ponytail, the tendrils
plastered wet and limp to her face.

Man, she was a worker.

"Okay," I said.

I bounced the ball to her, and we went at it again.
Then, after a drive and right-left fake, she uncorked another fade-away jump shot, this one off the mark. I think
she missed so she could out-hustle me for the rebound,
because she dashed for the basket before the shot was
hardly up. Both leaping high—she gained the better position—we stretched for the ball, and I snatched it off the
board, just above her fingertips.

I'm not sure what happened next. If we slipped or
what. All I know is we crashed to the concrete, arms and
legs tangled in a slippery, sweaty sprawl. *Splat!*

I lay there a second, the hot concrete burning my
back, her sweaty flesh sliding over mine. I was thinking,
"Wow!" I shoved her off me and sprang to my feet, my
heart pumping frantically. "Sorry," I said. "They don't call
me the Bruiser for nothing."

She sat up, her face twisted.

I just meant to reach down and help her up, like I had
when she sat under the oak tree. But when I pulled her to
her feet this time, she collapsed against me, her arms

around my neck, breasts spearing my chest, my arms around her waist.

My heart stopped. I'm not even sure I was breathing.

"It's my ankle," she gasped, and clung to me. "I think I broke my fucking ankle!"

I felt the wind go out of me, my knees weak. I could hardly hold her up.

Man, what do I do now?

6.

Angel wound her left arm around my neck, while my right one clenched her waist.

"I'm sorry, I'm sorry," I kept saying.

I helped her hobble to the basketball pole, where I eased her down so she could sit against it.

"I'll be okay." But Angel's face was scrunching up.

I crouched in front of her. "Your right ankle?"

She nodded. I untied her shoelace. She winced. "Shit!"

"Sorry," I said again.

I pulled off her shoe and sock. Held her calf in one hand, her sweaty foot in my other hand, a long foot, I thought, for a girl. No wonder she had such good balance.

"It's starting to swell," I said. "I can't tell if it's sprained or broken, but it's critical I get you home and we slap some ice on that, or it'll be as big as a balloon." I sounded like my dad.

"No, please. I'll get home by myself."

"How? You can't put an ounce of weight on that foot.

I'll drive my Jeep over here." I knew it was illegal to drive on the bike path and on the park grass, but this was an emergency.

"My bike," she said. "Someone will steal my bike." She pointed.

I hadn't seen her bike lying twenty feet away in the grass. No room for it in my Jeep.

I stood up, hands on my hips. Thought. Sweat dripped into my eyes, making them sting. What about the basketball? If I left it here, someone would steal it and the bike.

I scooped up the ball and hustled over to a tall blue spruce tree ten feet away that had never been trimmed, and hid the ball in the lower branches. On the way back, I picked up Angel's bike and wheeled it over to her.

"What are you doing?" she said.

"You live far from here?"

"A mile, mile and a half. I don't want you to take me home."

"I'm going to help you onto this bike, and I'm going to push you home."

"No." Stated flatly.

"This bike won't fit in my Jeep; you can't ride it or walk. You don't have a choice. And we've got to get ice on that ankle. You want me to leave you here?"

She didn't say another word, but I saw tears pooling in her eyes. The first girl I'd ever played basketball with, I'd broken or sprained her ankle, and now she was crying.

I hoisted Angel up, her arm around my neck. I bent a little at the knees, and picked up the bike. As I held the bike, she hopped around on one foot until she wiggled onto the seat, her hands clutching the handlebars.

I said, "Put your good foot on the pedal and let the other hang."

She did.

"Comfortable?" I said.

She nodded, but her jaw clenched.

"Hang on. Here we go."

My right hand clutching the back of the seat, my other on the handlebars, I pushed her slowly across the bumpy grass so as not to jar her bad ankle.

I eased into a left turn at the blacktop path and picked up my speed to an easy jog. The bike with Angel on it pushed like a feather. At first. The path was four feet wide and flat, which was good. But it was winding, following Duck Creek on our right, and that made it tough to stay on track. Its banks were full because of spring rains, and I could smell the muddy, roiling creek water. Lots of old willow trees grew on either side of the path, but they didn't provide any shade for us because the leaves hadn't fully blossomed yet, and I could feel the sun beating on me, slowing me down.

I figured I'd have Angel home in twelve minutes, fifteen. But that seemed like a lifetime. She needed ice on the swelling right now.

"How you doing?" I said.

"Okay. I wish you didn't have to do this."

"Still hurt?" Stupid question.

"Enough."

"The sooner we get that ankle iced, the better."

Two helmeted roller-bladers zoomed past us, their skates clacking.

Dripping sweat, I pushed Angel along in silence, listening to the slap of my Nikes on the path and the rasp of my own breathing.

"You don't have to run all the way," she said. "I'm not going to die."

"I'm okay."

I wasn't winded yet, but my legs were starting to feel limp, and I wondered how much farther, though I wasn't going to ask.

An older couple on bikes peddled toward us, and called, "Hello."

I puffed out a "Hi!"

"Not much farther," Angel said. A rabbit scooted out of the brush ten feet ahead, zipped across the path, and zigzagged for the creek bottom.

"Around the next bend is my backyard," Angel said. "You can stop there. I don't know how to thank you."

"Call me tonight, let me know how you're doing."

I pushed her around the bend, hoping this was the one she was talking about.

"Right here," Angel said. "I can make it the rest of the way."

I stopped, paused, caught my breath. Looked around. She'd have to struggle through a small grove of trees, then up the lawn to her house. No way.

"That your backyard?"

"Please. I can make it."

"If you had wings."

I pushed her through the trees, then up the gently sloping lawn to the back of her brick house and the concrete patio. The house had a walk-in basement.

"This is no good," I said. "If you go in through the basement, you'll have to climb up the stairs. I'll take you around front."

I expected another protest, but got only a terrible sigh and, "Why did this have to happen?"

As I pushed her around to the front of the house and onto the drive, I remembered Dad's telling me last night that playing basketball with a female was not a good plan. *First thing you know, you'd hurt her, then we'd get sued.*

"Is there anyone home?" I said.

As soon as that was out of my mouth, the garage's double-wide door rattled up, and there stood a small woman dressed in jeans and a white polo shirt, her gray hair cut short. She stood next to a red Grand Am, probably the same one I'd seen Angel climb into after school today. The other slot in the garage was empty.

She looked at Angel with bright, dark eyes, her face soft. "Is something wrong, sweetheart?"

"It's nothing," Angel said, teeth clenched.

"I was at the kitchen window and saw this young man pushing you on your bike."

I said, "We were playing basketball, Mrs. McPherson. We fell, and I think Angel's sprained her ankle. Maybe it's broken, I don't know. She needs to get some ice on it right away."

The woman's hand flew to her mouth. "Oh, my! Can you help her into the house?"

"He doesn't have to." Angel's voice was tight, her teeth pressed together. She was in real pain.

"Please get the door," I said.

Mrs. McPherson darted for the door, quick and jerky like a hummingbird. She didn't look or move anything like her graceful daughter.

I clamped onto Angel as she slid off the bike. Then I grabbed the bike by one hand and let it fall to the drive.

Angel's arm around my neck again, mine circling her waist, I helped her hop on one foot to the door, up one step, then into the kitchen.

Mrs. McPherson pulled out a chair. "Let her sit right there," she said. "I'll be back in a minute with crushed ice from the freezer in the basement." The woman vanished.

The kitchen smelled like cake or pie. Cookies, maybe. Something baking. No smells like that at my house. Ever.

I eased Angel onto the chair, knelt, and inspected her ankle. She threw her head back and squeezed her eyes shut.

"Oh, wow!" I said. "It is swelling. Right down to your toes. Does it hurt bad?"

"She's not my mother," Angel said to the ceiling.

"What?"

Soaked with sweat, I was dripping all over the linoleum floor.

"The woman you called Mrs. McPherson, she's not my mother. She's—" But the pain halted Angel. Her face twisted again, her lips stretched across her teeth.

"Who is she?"

I jerked my head around and realized the woman was standing in back of me with what appeared to be a five-pound plastic bag of crushed ice in her hands. She and Angel stared at each other.

"Crushed ice," I said. "Exactly what we need. You got a big bath towel or, better yet, an ice bag we can put some of this in?"

"We have an ice bag," the woman said.

"Bring a big towel, too," I said.

Dropping the ice in the sink, she dashed off.

Angel said, "She's my aunt. Aunt Diane. She's living with us for a while." Angel drew in a breath. "Ow! This damn thing hurts. It's starting to throb."

"Man, I'm sorry."

"Wasn't your fault."

Aunt Diane appeared with the ice bag, cap unscrewed, and a towel over her arm. At the sink, I punched a hole in the bag and filled the rubber ice bag with the crushed ice. I handed it to Aunt Diane.

I said, "You got a couch or a bed where Angel can lie down?"

"The living room."

"She's all sweaty."

"That's all right."

Without even a tiny complaint from Angel, I scooped her off the chair and carried her into a fancy living room. I didn't look around—no time—but I got the impression that lots of big furniture sat everywhere and plants perched all over the place. I laid Angel on a long plaid couch. She closed her eyes and gritted her teeth.

"We need two pillows," I said. "I'll take the ice bag and the towel."

Aunt Diane handed them to me and scooted away.

"You didn't need to do all this," Angel said. "You better get going."

"Trying to get rid of me? This is the least I can do."

I knelt and placed the bag on Angel's ankle. She flinched and bit her bottom lip.

Aunt Diane reappeared, a pink pillow under each arm. "Will these do?"

"Put one under her head," I said.

I took the other and patted it onto the arm of the couch, wrapped the towel around Angel's ankle and the ice bag, then lowered her foot onto the pillow.

"Keep your foot elevated," I told Angel. "That helps relieve the pain."

"Such a knowledgeable young man," Aunt Diane said.

I stood and cleared my throat. "My dad's a football coach. I've seen him deal with ankles, knees, and shoulders all my life. I've sprained my left ankle twice. Broke my right arm."

"Oh, my," Aunt Diane said. She looked at Angel. "Are you comfortable, sweetheart?"

"I'm okay."

"I don't know how to thank you, young man."

"Name's Danny Henderson," I said.

"Angel's mother will be home any minute now."

"Good," I said. "You should take her to the ER at Mercy and get some X-rays. It could be broken; it'll need a cast." I reached down and touched Angel's hand. "Call me, will you?"

I think she nodded yes, but I couldn't tell because, at that moment, a spasm of pain jolted her, and she screwed her whole face up tight, her mouth really crooked. She gripped my hand, then suddenly let it go.

"Maybe she needs a couple of Tylenol," I told Aunt Diane. "I've got to get going."

"Yes, of course. What did you say your name was?"

"Henderson. Danny Henderson. I can find my way out. Bye," I told Angel. "Call me."

I hurried out through the kitchen, and paused a moment in the neatly kept garage. Rakes, shovels, shears, and a hose hung on the walls. A lawn mower, snow blower, and gas can crouched in a corner. Two women's bikes, mounted on hooks, dangled from the ceiling rafters.

After picking up Angel's bike from the drive and wheeling it into the garage, I loped across the backyard down to the bike path, settling into a slow jog back to my Jeep, thinking something weird was going on. Angel kept insisting I not take her home, even though she knew she couldn't make it alone, and she seemed anxious to get me out of the house.

But all I had to do was put myself in her place, and I could see why she didn't want me to meet her mom. Maybe her mom didn't approve of guys like my dad didn't approve of girls. Maybe she'd told her mom she was doing something else this afternoon, like studying at the public library. How would she explain me? And why would she want to introduce her mom to the guy who had just messed up her ankle? That would be pretty stupid.

I pulled up at the basketball court. A bunch of yelling, screaming junior high boys were playing now, shirts and skins. They eyed me. They might have thought I was going to give them trouble. I sauntered over to the pine tree and pulled Angel's basketball out of the branches.

I bounced the ball in the grass as I headed toward the parking lot. A soft breeze blew across the open field, the smell of the creek in the air.

I couldn't wait for Angel's phone call tonight. Beautiful Angel. God, she turned me on. And then I wondered what damage I might have done to her basketball career.

7.

The next morning, I parked my Jeep on Waverly Road and trudged up the hill toward school. Slots in the school's overcrowded parking lot are awarded through a lottery each fall. Tony had been lucky enough to win a spot. Not me. I was forced to park on the street. I'd have to wait until next year to try again for my little slice of parking heaven.

It was a cloudy morning, chilly, the same way I felt.

Angel hadn't called last night. I hadn't called her, either. Though I'd found her number in the book, I couldn't make myself do it.

I crossed the parking lot, threading my way between parked cars and trucks, dodging kamikaze drivers trying to land on their pad. As usual, Tony was waiting for me in the cab of his Ranger.

I clicked the door open, hopped in, slammed the door. He glanced at the clock on the dash. "You're early."

"Guess what happened yesterday."

"History questions finished," he said, as he folded a piece of notebook paper and stuffed it inside his history book. Tucked a stubby pencil behind his ear. "What happened?"

I started off with meeting Angel in the park, working out with her, crushing her ankle, and ended with her not calling last night.

Tony shook his head and stacked his books on his lap, stowed his pencil under his seat. "Forget her. Let Melody fix you up. She's got friends dying to meet you."

"I'm not a charity case." I leaned my head back. "I figure Angel didn't call because when her mom got home, she rushed Angel to the ER at Mercy, but they had to wait for hours for a doctor to look at her. You know how that goes."

"You call her?"

"Couldn't make myself do it."

"Chicken."

I watched kids beginning to bail out of their cars and head for school.

I said, "The doctor couldn't put a cast on because the ankle was too swollen. And most likely he gave Angel pain pills, which, when she got home and settled, wiped her out, so she couldn't call." I gave a deep sigh. "She won't be in school today, either. She probably has to stay home until the swelling goes down and the doctor can put a cast on her ankle."

Tony looked at me. "You know what I figure? I figure your ass is grass, buddy. Dunlap's going to kill you."

"Dunlap didn't have anything to do with it."

"Duh! Remember, Miss Lee is Angel's coach? She's his

girlfriend. She'll bitch him out for letting an ape like you mangle her star."

"Think so?"

"I'll bet she nails Dunlap, he nails you, and either Dunlap or Lee—maybe both—goes straight to your dad. Did you tell him about hurting her?"

"Nothing."

"You're DOA, buddy!"

In first period Advanced Speech that morning, I knew the end was approaching. I expected it when a runner from the office delivered a yellow summons slip to my teacher, Miss Meier, at the end of the period. I thought for sure Dad was summoning me to his office. But then Miss Meier handed the slip to Patti Neal, and I thought I was safe, until the teacher dismissed us, and I found Dad standing in his red-and-white gym sweats in the hall, just outside my classroom door.

"Just the person I want to see," he said, his face red, as if he'd been running.

"I've got to get to World Cultures and stop by my locker."

"I need to talk to you."

"Dad—"

"In my office. Now."

It was a command I couldn't ignore.

I lagged behind Dad as I followed him down the hallway through the crush of students. I fell so far behind I lost sight of him. I didn't want kids thinking I was following my dad, like a puppy follows its master.

I thought about ditching. But why? He'd track me down again in seconds.

In his office, after he slammed the door, he pointed

to a chair in front of his gray metal desk and said, "Sit down."

He rates his own office, a small cubicle inside the boys' locker room, because he's head of the athletic department.

I sat and eased my books onto his desk.

His office smells like sweat, just like the locker room. I wondered if he ever notices it. A row of pictures of his football teams at BRH hangs on the wall, five pictures in all. I'm in two of them. An eight-by-eleven plaque honoring him as the Mississippi River Athletic Conference Coach of the Year last year hangs centered above the team pictures. He had a 10–2 record, and we went to state, but lost in the semifinals. Dad always says, "Next year, we'll win it all."

He stood behind his desk, working his lips. The fact that he was standing and I was sitting made me feel small, as if I'd shrunk.

"Tell me what the hell's going on." Calmly.

"What?" I said, trying to sound dumb. Not too difficult.

"You know who's been in here to talk to me this morning?"

I shook my head.

"You lied to me yesterday in the hallway, didn't you?" A bit louder, less calmly.

"I hardly saw you yesterday."

"I asked you if you were going to play basketball with that McPherson female."

"When we talked, I hadn't even seen her. I didn't know."

"But you had an idea you'd be seeing her. What the hell were you thinking?" He yanked the swivel chair out from behind his desk. Plopped down in it. The ceiling light glared off his head where he's growing bald on top.

He said, "I told you males and females aren't meant to compete against each other in sports. They're not made for it."

"Dad, it's a new century. Girls wrestle, play football and hockey. They box. They ride race horses, drive race cars."

He leaned back in his chair, rocking. Nodding. "You broke her ankle, are you aware of that?" Calmly again.

I closed my eyes a second. So it was true.

"It was an accident," I said, and bit my lip.

"I don't care what it was!" His palm slapped the desk. "You think her coach gives a damn that it was an accident? She was picked to participate on an all-star team this spring and travel to different states. It's not going to happen now."

I didn't know what to say. I started squeezing my hands. I couldn't have felt worse. "Did her mother call?" I said.

"Lee yelled at me this morning. She's the one who heard from the girl's mother. Dunlap marched in and gave me a bad time, too."

I stared at the ceiling. Took a breath. "We went up for a rebound. Somehow I must've come down on her ankle. I don't know, it just . . ." I stared at my hands in my lap as they clenched and unclenched.

"Look," Dad said, "it was an accident, accidents happen, we all know that." He slapped the desk again. "I'm mad because this one should not have happened. You should not have been playing basketball with her—I told you that."

"She showed me a lot of good stuff about free-throw shooting."

He snorted. "I already have enough trouble with that prima donna coach of hers, Miss Susan Lee. She's never satisfied with the times I assign to her for practice in the gym. Now this!" Dad scribbled my name with a ballpoint on his pad of hall passes. Ripped one off and thrust it at me. "Get to class."

I stood up and gathered my books. "I'm sorry, Dad."

He rubbed his palm across the top of his head. His face smoothed out. "Look, Chief, I don't care what they say, it's a man's world. The fewer females you allow into your life, the fewer problems you'll have."

I'll bet he's told me that a million times.

I nodded. "Seems like it."

Tony surprised me during A lunch. He has B lunch, a split lunch, which means he starts class, goes to lunch, then back to finish the same class. But here he was, elbowing his way into line in front of two skinny, complaining fresh-man nerds who were right behind me.

"You can't cut," one of them whined.

"Eat shit and die," Tony said, and they cowered away.

"What's up, man?" I said.

"We've got a speaker for World Cultures all week. Scott doesn't want to split class, so he's giving us A lunch. What's happening?"

"It's worse than I imagined."

I filled my tray with spaghetti, French bread, salad, or-ange Jell-O, and chocolate milk. School lunches aren't that bad.

We navigated to my favorite corner table, where we could have some privacy, if not quiet. Before I could even shovel in a mouthful of food, I said, "You were right. Lee went straight to my dad and complained."

Tony nodded. Broke open his milk carton, took a gulp.

I said, "The worst part is, Angel was supposed to play on an all-star team this spring. I shot that down." I dug into my spaghetti.

"Not to worry, buddy. Melody's going to line you up with Bambi Powers."

"If Angel just wouldn't have taken that last shot—"

"Are you listening to me?" Tony said. "Maybe the four of us could go to the prom together. Be more fun if you came along. Melody spends half her time in the restroom."

"The prom?" I blinked. I hadn't thought about the prom. I'm not really a prom kind of person.

"Bambi's not blond, I realize you must like blonds. She's that redheaded cheerleader. You've seen her, she's hot. She and Melody are buddy-buddy."

"She's not for me."

"It's about time you went to one dance with a girl."

Tony lifted a forkful of spaghetti to his mouth, but halted it in midair. His eyes got big, and he set his fork down. "Watch out," he said. "Behind you."

Before I could turn around, I felt a square paw on my shoulder, squeezing my neck, making me wince. I recognized the grip right away. Not my dad's—Dunlap's.

I twisted my neck, scrunched my shoulders. He let go, and I peered up at him, feeling the blood drain from my face. He's six-eleven, skinny, and hawk-nosed. Some of his players—not me—even call him Hawk-face. But only behind his back.

"I know you agreed to shoot against Angel McPherson in the assembly," he said, "but when did you decide to take her to a park and maul her?"

"I didn't maul her."

"Next time, Danny boy, pick on someone your own size. What were you thinking of?"

"Basketball. Is Miss Lee mad at me, too?"

"Not at you. She figures football players are too dumb to know any better, but she's mad at Angel. The girl should've had more smarts. She works harder than anybody else on the basketball team, and now she's ruined her opportunity to play against the best competition in the Midwest this summer, and to step up her game, build her reputation for college scouts. Why the hell did you step on her?"

Tony tried to rescue me. "It was an accident, Coach."

Dunlap nodded. Patted my back. "Tell you what. I don't know what your intentions are, Danny, but just stay away from Angel, okay? Find someone else."

"That," Tony said, "is what I've been trying to tell him."

Dunlap crouched a little, as if to speak confidentially. "This doesn't have to go any farther. The girl's a talented athlete, nobody denies that, but she's got some problems. Personal ones, you know. Don't make any more waves. That's all I can say. Leave her alone." Dunlap straightened. "Got it?"

"Got it," I said.

After Dunlap left, I stared at my food, pissed that everyone was trying to tell me what to do.

"Bambi Powers is looking better all the time," Tony said. "What about the pig roast Saturday? You're cooking—ask her to that."

"I wouldn't touch her with a ten-foot pole," I said. "I'm not giving up on Angel McPherson."

8.

At supper that night, over gizzards from Kentucky Fried Chicken—Dad and I love them—he said, "Been thinking maybe you should get a job this summer. Teach you something about handling money. Budgeting."

It was raining hard, not a good night for barbecuing outside, so Dad had paid a visit to the Colonel.

We always have salad with the gizzards, along with KFC's mashed potatoes and gravy. Dad used to be able to eat many more gizzards than I could, but not any longer. I couldn't comment right away because my mouth was full.

I swallowed. "Sounds like a good idea," I said. I swallowed again. Took a gulp of milk. "Maybe I can get a job with the city road crew. Tony's dad's got pull."

"You could work at Eagle or Hy-Vee. I understand those grocery stores are good about scheduling kids around school activities." He drank some Old Style. Split a gizzard in two with his knife and fork. Ate thoughtfully. "You could quit during football season, then go back. You wouldn't have to play basketball if you didn't want to. Have a whole winter of employment. Save some money for college. Give up basketball."

I felt his eyes on me, watching for my reaction. I knew what he was thinking. I'd lived with him long enough. Keep the kid busy. Job, weight lifting, golf, football camp, fishing—he won't have time for basketball this summer. Or females.

"Basketball's okay," I said. I waltzed the last gizzard around my plate with my fork. Dipped it in gravy. "I'm not ready to drop the game. Besides, you've always told me to finish things I start."

He nodded, and we ate in silence for a while. I got up to get more gizzards from the pan on the stove. Dad always dumps them out of the KFC cardboard tub into a hot frying pan so he can get the batter on the outside crispy. I like them like that.

I sat down again.

Dad said, "Football is what you need to concentrate on, Chief. Forget about outside shooting and free throws. You could use some more work in the weight room. You were all-conference last season, maybe all-state this year. Your grades could be better, but you'll still get plenty of scholarship offers. Don't lose sight of your goals."

Your goals, Dad.

Dad finished off his Old Style, tipping the can back for the last drop. He set the can down carefully on the table. Wiped off his mouth with a napkin. Rain beat on the kitchen windows.

"I'm telling you something else," he said. "It's not a good idea to hang around with Angel McPherson this summer, if that's what's on your mind."

I kept my face blank. "Who said anything about that?"

"You've already gotten into trouble once because of her." He shoved his chair back. "Get a job if you want. Spend your free time in the weight room this summer. And don't forget our summer fishing trip. But forget about basketball and Angel McPherson."

He stood up. That was his final word on the matter.

"I'll clear things away," I said.

Not much to do. Throw away the paper plates, stuff our salad bowls and silverware into the dishwasher, toss the KFC debris out. Wipe off the table. I finished in five minutes.

Dad and I were so much alike in some ways, I was practically his clone. But what would you expect, living together alone all this time, seventeen years. And we'd had lots of fun together.

Dad was generous with good times. Like that fishing trip he'd just mentioned. Every year come early August, Dad and I and about six other guys, all friends of his on the faculty, go to northern Wisconsin to fish. We live in pop-up campers and tents. We fish all day for crappie, bass, walleye, northern, and muskie; come in sunburned. We clean the fish, then fix a giant supper, stuffing ourselves with deep-fried fillets.

After doing dishes, we sit around and build the cooking fire into a blazing campfire and swap stories about the day's fishing adventures. You can't tell the lies from the truth. By nine o'clock, I'm so exhausted I stagger into my bunk in the camper and climb, totally zonked, into my sleeping bag until sunrise. I never even hear the raccoons fighting at night over the food we might've left out by mistake, but everybody else talks about them in the morning.

When I was younger, I wanted those times to go on forever, and I wanted to be exactly like my dad. Now I like fishing with Tony, not with my dad's friends. I like the Cubs and the Bears. Dad likes the Cardinals and the Lions. And I don't much like shooting things anymore: turkey, pheasant, deer. I've never said anything, though.

I worked on my chemistry homework in my bedroom, listening to the rain in the background. About nine o'clock, I crept down the basement steps to check on Dad. He slumped, asleep in his lounge chair in front of the flickering colored light of the TV screen, head tipped to one side, snoring softly. I crept back upstairs. From the den, I snatched the cordless, marched to my room, and closed the door.

Flopping onto my bed on my back, my heart racing, I dialed Angel McPherson's number, then snapped off the light on the night table.

I held in a breath when she answered after the second ring.

"Hi," I said. "This is Danny. How you doing?" The plastic phone felt warm in my palm.

"I'm fine, Danny. I was just getting ready to call you."

"Big cast on your ankle?"

"Not very."

I rolled onto my side. "I wish I knew something magic to make your ankle better. Sorry about your missing that all-star league."

"How'd you know?"

"Dunlap mentioned it today. I feel rotten. You're on crutches, obviously?"

"For three or four weeks. Then a walking cast for a couple of weeks. First broken bone ever."

"Six weeks," I said. "Wow. This is terrible."

"It's not so bad. Everybody's waiting on me."

I could see Angel's aunt and mom fussing over her, helping her with her crutches, fetching a drink for her. I'd never had a mom to fuss over me.

"Sorry I didn't call last night. The doctor gave me pain pills, and they knocked me out."

I rolled onto my back again. "Figured that."

"I get to go to school tomorrow."

"Good."

A pause. In the darkness, the rain seemed to pelt my bedroom windows louder than before.

I said, "You still there?"

"Yes."

"I've got to do weight training for football, but I've made up my mind I'm going to commit most of my summer to improving my basketball shooting skills. You think you can still help me?"

"Why not? In fact, I'll have a lot more time. You know what you need to do?"

"What?"

"Develop an organized daily workout plan and stick to it. I'll bet in six weeks, you'll be amazed at your improvement. That is, if you're serious."

"I am. Honest, I am."

"When did you start playing?"

"Junior high, because I was bigger than anybody else, and the coach recruited me out of gym class. All I had to do was shove people around. That worked till I made the varsity this year."

"You need to practice more."

I said I'd take her home from school tomorow, wait for her while she changed, then we could go to the park, and I could learn under her watchful eye. She balked at that, giving all kinds of excuses. She clearly didn't want me hanging around her house, so I asked if she could get someone to bring her to the park, and I'd take her home. Drop her off at the curb in front of her house.

"I think that'll work," she said, and we decided on four o'clock.

"I've still got your basketball," I said.

"Bring it."

"When your ankle gets better, I can show you some things about blocking out and rebounding. How to hook elbows. Step on toes and heels and pull on jerseys. How to fake taking an elbow in the nose. Or how to give one and make it look like an accident."

She laughed, and my heart melted at the sound.

"Do you know any legal moves?" she said.

"A few."

We talked another half hour about favorite movies, TV programs, and music. She likes soaps, sitcoms, romantic comedies, and blues. I hate all that. I like sports, nature programs, action/adventure, and country.

We talked and laughed until we were tired, and finally hung up. In the inky darkness, I stripped down to my jockey shorts, left my clothes in a pile on the floor, and climbed into bed. I guess a mom would've chewed me out for not at least washing my face and hands and brushing my teeth before I went to bed.

I lay on my back, hands laced under my head, listening to the rain tap on my windows.

I didn't know how long I could keep Angel McPherson a secret from Dad. Or what I'd say when he found out.

9.

The next morning, as usual, Tony slouched in his truck in the school parking lot as I popped in, sat next to him, and slammed the truck door. He'd finished his homework. I was late. The rain had stopped sometime during the night, and now the sun was spreading an orange glow across a cloudless blue sky, but the weatherman had promised more rain for later today.

I told Tony the latest between Angel and me, and he said, "Give her up, buddy."

"The biggest problem I'm going to have," I said, "is my dad. I mean, I'd like to meet her by her locker. I could get a hall pass to help her out. Haul her books and stuff. She's on crutches, you know."

"Melody and I have talked this over," he said, "and if you don't like Bambi Powers, there's Lori Fisher. Beautiful babe, but she's a brunette."

I frowned. "Forget it. I need to figure out how to avoid my dad in the halls."

Cars and trucks zoomed by, exhaust thick in the air, tires screeching.

Tony said, "I'm going to tell you something, buddy. Maybe it's just an ugly rumor, but you have the right to know."

"What?"

He looked away from me, out the windshield. "You're being taken for a ride. Angel's gay."

First my mouth dropped open. Then I stared at him, but he wouldn't look at me. Next, I laughed at him. "That is ugly. Where'd you get your information?"

"Melody."

"How does Melody know? She see Angel with somebody?"

Tony glanced at the dash clock. "Got to make tracks, man, we're going to be late for sure."

"Lunchtime," I said, grabbing at the door handle. "I want to see you at lunchtime."

"Lunchtime."

All morning in my classes, I laughed at the idea. Angel, gay. How did such a rumor get started? But a person has to beware of rumors. Sometimes they're true. Dad had heard rumors about Mom and ignored them for a long while, he told me, but they turned out to be true. Mom was having an affair, and her sister was providing her with a place to meet her lover.

Dad's own mom had been the same way with her husband. Unfaithful. He told me about Grandma once when we sat alone around a campfire. He had had too many beers. He never mentioned her again. His mom, his sister-in-law, his wife—women who had betrayed him. Easy to understand why Dad hates females.

All my grandparents are dead now.

At lunch in the cafeteria, I sat across the table from Tony and Melody. Tony had dragged her into the cafeteria to eat with us. She usually brought a sack lunch and ate with her cheerleader buddies in a corner of the gym. After cramming their lunches down, whatever time they had left, they spent polishing routines. Cheerleading is a pretty competitive business.

"Tell him," Tony said to Melody, without any preliminaries.

"What?" she said, and dug in her brown paper bag for a sandwich, then frowned, swiping her long black hair out of her eyes. "Man, my mom gives me tuna sandwiches at least twice a week—because *she* likes it."

Tony said, "What you told me yesterday, tell him."

Melody studied me with her dark eyes and licked her lips, always a deep red. "It's just a rumor, but I think it's true. I mean, I'm in gym class with Angel McPherson, and I cheered at all her games. She's weird, you know."

"Tell him everything," Tony said.

I opened my carton of milk and took a giant bite of my hot dog. Followed it with a gulp of milk.

"She doesn't hang with anybody. Doesn't go to parties. Her mom and this other lady—she looks like a dyke—were together at her championship game in Des Moines."

I wiped my mouth with a napkin. "That's her aunt. So what?"

Melody shrugged. "You can just tell, you know. You can tell. She doesn't wear jewelry or makeup. No finger-nail polish."

I set my hot dog down on my tray and stared at Melody. I liked her, even though she was bossy, opinion-ated, and had totally pussy-whipped Tony. But this was too much.

"So you started a rumor," I said, "that Angel's gay, on the basis that you can just tell that she is? She doesn't wear jewelry, makeup, or nail polish."

"I didn't start it, Danny. All us girls feel the same way. Marie, Annie, Grace, Jennifer, Emily, Roxanne, Bambi— all of us. We've talked about it. The girls on the basketball team feel the same way. They don't even like to shower with her."

Tony, I noticed, was staying out of this conversation. The Fox, hiding in his den.

Melody had nibbled half her tuna sandwich down and was now peeling an orange.

I said, "Because Angel doesn't go ape over every jock, you can tell she's gay. Is that what you're saying?"

"Could be," Tony chimed in, between dipping spoon-fuls of chili into his mouth.

Melody said, "Danny, Bambi's had a crush on you for two years. Prom's coming up soon. Five weeks."

"I doubt if you'll see me at the prom."

"There's the pig roast Saturday. Ricky Allen's birthday party. Ask her."

I said, "I'm not stupid, you know. I see what's hap-pening here. You guys want me to go out with Bambi Powers, so you're trying to convince me that the girl I re-ally like is a lesbian."

"Prove she's not," Tony said. "Ask her to Saturday's pig roast. See how close you can get to her, buddy."

"Probably as close as I want. I can't believe you guys would try to scam me, try to make me think Angel's gay, so I'll go out with Bambi." I shook my head. "Nice friends I've got."

"She thinks you're a stud," Melody said. "She's watched you play every game. Football and basketball."

"So what?"

"I'll tell you what." Melody seemed to be getting a little pissed. "She knows you're the only studly looking guy in this school who hasn't tried to screw every girl who even looks half alive."

"Who told her that?"

"I did, Danny. I like her. I'm trying to do both of you a favor here."

"Even girls like to nail a virgin," Tony said. "That's why she wants you. Ever think of that? Let it happen, man."

I shook my head. "If I ask anyone," I said, "I'll ask Angel McPherson."

"A lesbian on crutches," Tony said, "and a horny football player with two left feet—anything wrong with that picture?"

"Call Bambi," Melody said, "before someone else does."

I shook my head again. Angel was too beautiful to be gay. Never in a million years would I change my mind about her. Melody, Bambi, Tony, my dad—all of them were wasting their time.

10.

I wheeled my Jeep into the parking lot at 3:55. Angel was sitting alone at a picnic table ten feet away, her crutches propped beside her against the bench.

Taking a sharp right, I maneuvered into a parking space in front of her.

The day had turned into one of those gray days in spring when the sun bursts through for five minutes, only to be blotted out again by dark clouds, threatening rain, just as the weatherman had predicted.

Did I have the guts to ask Angel to Saturday's pig roast? Why not? She must like me. Even though I'd broken her ankle, she was meeting me here. Hadn't I gathered enough courage to ask her for help with my free-throw shooting?

The second I jumped out of the Jeep, the sun punched its way through the clouds.

I reached behind the passenger's seat in the Jeep for the basketball, palmed it, and walked over to the table. She sat on the other side.

"Hi," I said.

"Right on time," she said, and flashed me a smile.

Man, she knocked me out. No way is this girl gay!

"Let me see your cast." I skirted the picnic table.

She wore jean shorts and a baggy white sweatshirt. She swiveled around and thrust out her right leg, resting it on the bench. Climbing halfway up her calf, her cast was deep pink.

"I've never seen that color before. Only white."

"Designer casts. Any color you want. Purple. Black. Red. All you need is a broken bone to qualify."

I couldn't believe how upbeat she sounded.

"Hurt?" I said.

"Not much. Cast makes me feel clumsy, but I'm okay."

I sat across from her, dropping the ball to the ground.

"So you're serious about improving your basketball game," she said.

I nodded. "I'm dedicated."

A breeze blew, and she brushed her hair from her face.

"Why all of a sudden? Why now?" she said.

Because I'm crazy about you.

"I play so I have something to do during the winter. Keeps me in shape. I rebound, pop in a few layups, wait for Tony to throw me the ball—I do okay. Eleven points a game."

"You're lazy."

That hurt a little. I frowned. "I wasn't interested in expanding my game until"—I looked at her with a level gaze—"until I saw how good you are and how easy you make shooting look, and I said, 'Man, I can do that!'" My next thought raced into my head and out of my mouth before I could stop it. "Besides," I said, "I think you're cool. Somebody I'd like to know better."

I sat motionless, my hands clasped on the table, my heart at a standstill. I hadn't intended to lay myself on the line like that. I could get laughed at. Stomped on.

Was she embarrassed? I was.

"Sorry," I said. "Just babbling."

She gave me the tiniest smile and reached across the table to touch my hand with her fingertips. "I think you're cool, too, Danny. . . ." But I noticed she didn't say

I was someone she'd like to know better. Then her face broke into a wide grin. "But you're a lousy free-throw shooter, and as a perimeter shooter, you stink." From beside her on the bench, she produced a clipboard with papers snapped to it. She pulled a sheet loose and handed it to me. "Take a look at this progress chart."

I studied the sheet. It was pretty basic. It had a place for the date, time, how many shots I took, how many I made, and my percentage. It had columns labeled "Excellent," "Good," "Fair," and "Poor." I was supposed to rate myself on shot fundamentals, like "Toes Pointed at the Basket."

"What are you going to do with this?" I asked.

"I'll give you a bunch of charts, and you can rate yourself when you practice. Whenever we get together, I'll watch your shooting, then rate you myself. We'll compare."

I must have been frowning again.

"What's wrong?" she said. "You're serious, aren't you?"

"This is something you'd give a junior high kid."

"That's where your skill level is, Danny."

I opened my mouth to protest.

Before a word escaped, she said, "If you don't think so, why aren't you shooting eighty percent at the line, or better? You've got the physical capabilities. Look at you."

She had me there.

She said, "You have to pay attention to these tiny details until you don't have to think about them anymore. That's your first step."

I carried the ball and the clipboard, and Angel glided along beside me on her crutches, taking smooth strides, not hobbling, like you see most people doing on crutches. I had to hustle to keep up.

The clouds had out-dueled the sun, the sky once again gray, a little chill in the air powered by a breeze.

While Angel stood on her crutches or sometimes leaned against the basketball pole, I practiced free throws. She whipped a counter out of her pocket and clicked off each shot I took. When I reached a hundred, she said, "All right, that's enough. I see improvement already. Your shot's much smoother. Seventy out of a hundred. Not bad for a muscle-bound football player." She smiled. "Let's try some outside shooting."

"Yes, sir!" I said, and she smiled again.

I didn't feel comfortable with my jump shot at all. No rhythm. I felt mechanical. I could smack a golf ball, blast a baseball, flatten a tennis ball, hurl a bowling ball. But this shooting thing with a basketball required more touch than power. That was my problem. Touch.

Angel kept telling me, "Elbow under the ball, follow through. Remember the bird's nest! Reach inside it for an egg."

"The wind is blowing some of my shots off target," I complained, after a third miss in a row.

"Good shooters never make excuses."

Who is this person?

Then I canned four in a row and was feeling pretty good about myself.

The rain came all at once, chilling me through my sweaty T-shirt, big fat drops, a downpour, threatening to drench us on the spot.

No point in dashing under a tree. No leaves to catch the rain. My Jeep was at least a hundred yards away. Our best shot was a picnic shelter thirty yards deeper into the park.

I snatched the clipboard out of Angel's hand so she wouldn't have to mess with it. Then I hightailed after the basketball, which had bounded away in the opposite direction.

When I reached the shelter, Angel sat perched atop a picnic table, left foot on the seat, right leg stretched straight, crutches propped beside her.

I sank down next to her on the table and shivered, a chill streaking through me. I dropped the basketball, and it rolled off the concrete pad into the grass. I set the clipboard behind me.

"My teeth are chattering," Angel said.

"Mine, too. I wish we had a blanket or something."

"Ten guys standing under an umbrella," Angel said, and grinned. "How many got wet?"

I thumped my forefinger on my head. "That's an old one! I know that. Wait!"

"None! It wasn't raining!" Angel rocked back with laughter.

"No fair! You didn't wait."

"You've got to be quick, Danny."

As the rain pounded the metal roof above us, I wiggled closer to Angel. Our arms touched, our legs. Her warmth felt good.

She peered at her outstretched leg and said, "I'm not supposed to get my cast wet."

"Man, I forgot about that. This kind of rain won't last long, though. Then we can go back to the Jeep."

We were silent a moment. Then she said, "You've lived here all your life?"

"My dad and I are from Michigan. Saginaw, Michigan. When he was a kid, he worked in the Vlasic pickle factory. I always think of that when I eat pickles."

"I always think of Florida when I eat oranges now. My dad used to bring me stuffed animals. The first one was a parrot, like you see flying wild in Florida. I have tons of stuffed animals. I still collect them. They always make me think of him."

"Why'd you come here—up North—to a climate like this?"

"My mom's decision."

I expected Angel to say more, but when she didn't, I said, "My dad applied for the head football coaching job here and got it; that was five years ago. You have a bunch of relatives in Florida?"

"I have only my mom."

I looked at her. "What about your aunt?"

She was peering at the rain, her face expressionless. For a second, I didn't think she was going to answer. Then, "Yes, there's my aunt."

"Your boyfriend taking you to the prom?"

She shook her head. "I don't have a boyfriend."

"You're beautiful, Angel. The guys at school should be hustling you all the time."

"I'm not beautiful," she said quietly. "I hate it when people say that." Her voice had an edge to it, but when she turned to look at me, her face softened.

"You're cold, aren't you?" I said, and my heart began beating like a hammer in my chest. I wanted to loop my arm around her and pull her close. Keep her warm. Kiss her.

She swallowed.

"It's all right if you kiss me," she whispered, as her eyes flicked away from mine. "That's what you're think-ing, aren't you? You want to kiss me."

I sucked in a breath. "Yes," I said. A croak. "I want to kiss you."

"You go first."

I leaned forward, breathing in the scent of her rainy hair. A sweet brushing of lips. But as she murmured,

"Hmm . . .," her breath warm against my mouth, she circled her arm around my neck, and I discovered a deeper flavor, sweet as thick honey. Our kissing threatened to melt me on the spot.

I'm not sure when the rain stopped. Somehow I heard the silence above our breathing and my pounding heart. I released her, looked at her, and slid off the picnic table. I ducked through the rain dripping off the shelter's roof and peered upward. The clouds had broken apart, and the sun had powered its way to the front again.

I stuffed my hands into my jean pockets. I glanced at her. Her face was flushed a light pink.

"We better go," I said.

I handed the crutches to her. I gathered up the clipboard and basketball, and we navigated the soggy grass toward my Jeep. In a few steps, my feet were soaked, squishing in my Nikes. A cardinal was wailing its brains out loud and clear in a nearby treetop.

I didn't know what to say or do now. Kissing Amber Clarke had never been like this, leaving me limp and on fire at the same time. I wondered how Angel would rate me if she'd had a progress chart for kissing. I'd have given her a ten on any kind of chart.

I still hadn't asked her to the pig roast.

Silence. The ride to her house would take only a minute or two.

As I backed out of my parking spot, she studied the top sheet on her clipboard.

"This got wet from the rain," she said. "I have to make a new one."

"Be kind," I said, my first words. Brilliant.

When I parked in front of her house, the sun still shining, she handed me the top sheet and five or six others. I shoved them under my seat.

"That should be enough till I see you again," she said.

Ask her, stupid! But I suddenly thought maybe I was moving too fast. We'd only met twice in the park, and already I was kissing her. I should pace myself. Give her a chance to catch her breath. Timing was everything.

"I'll call you tonight," I said.

She shook her head. "Please don't. My crutches?"

I hopped out of the Jeep, dragged her crutches out, and circled to her side.

"I'll help you to the door," I said. "Give me the clipboard."

"I can manage." She tucked the clipboard behind the waistband of her cutoffs.

Her telling me not to call didn't make any sense, so I said again, "I'll call," and handed her crutches to her.

She stared down at her cast. "Not tonight, Danny."

"Well, then call me. Anytime. Okay?" I didn't care if Dad answered or not. Eventually, I'd have to tell him flat-out that Angel and I were—what? Basketball buddies? Kissing buddies? Or were we?

"All right," she said. "I will."

I wanted to kiss her once more. Maybe that was the thing to do. Kiss her, then ask her. Strike instantly. Before she could catch her breath. But she must've seen my lips puckering or something, because she said quickly, "See you," and swung around on her crutches.

She'd made two smooth strides up the walk toward her porch when I said it. I'll bet she never expected it—I didn't. "Will you go to a pig roast this Saturday afternoon? Big birthday party on the Wapsi River."

I held my breath. In fact, I couldn't breathe. Here I was again, laying myself on the line. Would she laugh at me this time? Stomp on me?

She stopped so suddenly I thought she might fall face

first, smacking her nose on the concrete. Squaring her shoulders, she thrust her crutches forward, took another step with her left foot, and marched up the walk to the front porch. As if by magic, the front door opened, and Aunt Diane appeared in the doorway, pushing open the screen door. Without turning around or looking back over her shoulder, without answering me or saying good-bye, Angel hoisted herself up the three porch steps and into the house.

I climbed into my Jeep and sat behind the wheel for a minute or two. Had my timing been that far off? I started the Jeep, crunched it into gear, and squealed the tires as I drove away.

I hadn't been laughed at or stomped on. I'd been ignored. I'd fouled out when I thought I'd made a brilliant play. A three-point basket. But she'd whistled me to the bench.

She'd said it was okay if I kissed her, but had refused my invitation for a date. She'd said yes, then no.

What was that all about?

11.

Ricky Allen's folks own a summer camp on the Wapsi River, and they chaperoned the pig roast, along with two or three other adults. Ricky is a center on the football team and a heavyweight wrestler. He invited about twenty, twenty-five kids. He knew others would crash the party, but he didn't care.

My dad's hog roaster is a fifty-gallon oil drum split lengthwise, with an electric motor and an old stoker gearbox welded on one end to turn the spit. The top half of the drum is welded on hinges to the bottom half, so the roaster has a lid that you can open and close. The whole thing is mounted on a cut-down boat trailer, complete with turn signals and license plates. You can haul the roaster around and have a party wherever you want. I'd helped Dad roast hogs for the last-day-of-school faculty parties and for the Elks' family picnics.

Naturally I was elected to do the cooking.

Allen's Grove, a few miles out of town, is a perfect party spot. Oaks, cottonwoods, willows, sycamores, and hickory trees surround the area on three sides, the Wapsi River cutting across in front.

By ten in the morning, kids were blasting volleyballs, slugging softballs, and tossing horseshoes. By eleven, I had the hog rotating on a spit, crackling and sputtering to a golden crust over a charcoal fire in the bottom of the roaster. The hog weighed 190 pounds dressed—a monster from Johnnie's Meat Market. Johnnie himself had delivered it, and I'd towed the cooker out to Allen's Grove with my Jeep.

The day, the mood, the place—everything was perfect except for one major flaw. Angel wasn't there. I hadn't talked to her or seen her for over a week.

Why hadn't she answered me when I'd asked for a date? What had those kisses been all about? Nothing? Was she truly made of stone? I hated feeling all twisted up inside. Is this the way females treated guys? I figured the ball was in her court, the next move was hers, but she hadn't made one. And neither had I. No meeting at school. No telephone call. Hadn't she said she'd call me? Nothing. I'd already humiliated myself once by asking her out, then getting ignored. I wasn't going to do that again.

Maybe it was too much for her to handle. Time for her to back out of our brief relationship. Time for me to back off. Maybe she *was* gay.

Wipe her out of your memory, Danny. Try another girl. But on that sunny morning, while I was roasting the pig, I kept hoping somehow she would appear from the blue sky, and we'd spend an afternoon and evening together on the river.

About two in the afternoon, Bambi Powers and Pete Stinocher strutted up to where I was cooking the pig, next to the cabin. The bounce in Bambi's step advertised that she was braless under her tank top, the fine white cloth outlining her most excellent breasts, nipples poking through, as if they were staring at me.

A whole pig roasting on a spit isn't an everyday sight. Everyone wanders over at least once. The really curious ask how much it weighs, when I started cooking it, when it will be done.

Stinocher, a senior, and I had a long-standing rivalry, both of us playing tight end on the varsity football team. I'm bigger, but he's quicker, yet not as fast—there's a difference. Dad made me the starting tight end this year and moved Stinocher to defense, linebacker, which he hated, though outwardly we remained semifriendly.

I'd just opened the roaster lid to pour in more charcoal. Stinocher peered through the heavy blue smoke rolling out of the cooker at the rotating hog. Melting fat dripping onto the charcoal creates a smoke rich with a pork smell.

"Looks like you're doing a great job," he said. A chew bulging in his left cheek, he spit in front of my feet on the grass. Two inches from my new Red Wing boots.

I eyed him. Shifted my feet.

"When did you start?" he said.

"Six this morning."

"Where'd you get a whole pig?" Bambi smiled at me, dark eye shadow and mascara highlighting her green eyes. Her red hair was cut short. All curls. Angel's hair is long. Flowing. Blond.

"Johnnie's Meat Market," I said.

Bambi stuffed her hands into the pockets of her cutoff jeans, which were snipped so short the pockets hung out. "You can smell it a mile away. Smells good. Where's the head?"

"Sawed off," I said.

She made a face, wrinkling a tiny nose above full lips, colored with plum-dark lipstick. "Gross."

"When will it be done?" Stinocher said.

"Before dark."

"How do you know when it's done?" Bambi said.

"Meat thermometer right there in the shoulder. It's done when the thermometer reads one-eighty."

Stinocher nodded and spit again in front of my feet. Not as close this time. "Catch you later, man."

Bambi flipped her head, tossing her gold earrings.

"Later, Danny," she said, and smiled at me again.

"Later."

I watched her saunter away, her butt wiggling in her cutoffs.

I needed to avoid her.

From behind, someone slapped me on the shoulder. "Take a good look at her, buddy? She wants your body."

It was Tony, holding hands with Melody.

"Pretty nice," I said, and cast a final glance Bambi's way. "But not my type."

I closed the lid on the cooker before the grease dripping on the charcoal caught fire. If that happened, I'd be in big trouble. I wiped my hands on a rag from my back pocket.

"I told her you were looking for someone to go to the prom with," Melody said.

"Looks like Stinocher's got a lock on Bambi," I said.

"Can't tell," Tony said.

"I'm telling you," Melody said, "she likes you."

I shrugged, and Tony gave me a disgusted look.

About six, sooner than I expected, the hog was ready to come off the spit, a greasy job. Not much carving to it. The hog was so done it fell apart and melted in your mouth, juicy and smoky-sweet with a hickory flavor from the chips I'd added to the fire. We ate the meat on buns with barbecue sauce and onions. And baked beans, potato salad, coleslaw, deviled eggs—things everyone brought.

At dusk, Tony started a fire close to the riverbank, smoky and flickering at first, until the flames dried the damp wood, then suddenly bright, leaping against the darkening timberline.

The night turned sweatshirt-chilly with a million stars in the sky, so close I felt I could touch them. A giant moon looked too big to hang in the sky without falling.

I wished again Angel were here. Even if the ball was in her court, I should've called her. Found out what was wrong. Asked her again to the pig roast.

Finishing my sandwich, I dumped my paper plate into a trash barrel. I cleaned off Dad's carving knives and forks, packed them away, and hooked the cooker to the Jeep's trailer hitch. Dad always does those chores, right after eating.

A keg iced in a tub sat on the tailgate of Harvey

Spear's pickup, parked near the edge of the woods. Dad would have had a fit if he knew there was beer here. The adult chaperones sitting around the fire singing with a bunch of kids were either blind, didn't care, or were afraid to break up the fun. They wanted to be good guys. Dad hates those kinds of parents.

Hanging in a tree from a limb above the truck, a Coleman lantern lit the shiny faces of fifteen or twenty kids clustered around Spear's vehicle as if it were a watering hole in the desert. I grabbed a plastic cup off the truck's tailgate, and looked into the bright eyes of Bambi Powers.

"Hi," she said, and smiled. "Getting a beer?"

I nodded and smiled back.

"Get me one," she said. "It's for Pete. I get all foam."

"Sure."

Bambi handed me a cup. She was wearing Stinocher's red-and-white letter jacket. The sleeves dipped down past her fingertips. Her red hair shone like fire in the lantern light.

I said, "You've got to tilt the cup, open the spigot all the way, and let the beer run down the side. That's the secret."

I handed her the beer and drew one for myself.

"You're an expert," she said.

"You want one, too?"

"No, thanks."

"You guys gonna drink it dry?" someone squawked behind me, tapping me on the shoulder.

"Sorry," I said, peering down at a zit-faced kid.

"Let's get out of here," Bambi said.

I elbowed my way through the crowd and strolled aimlessly across the grassy yard, sipping my beer, Bambi trailing close behind. Laughing, shoulder-bumping kids sat on logs that circled the fire. They'd kept the blaze roaring, flames leaping hot and red into the sky, casting restless shadows across the yard.

Bambi made me nervous. I stopped, cleared my throat. "Where's Stinocher?"

"In the cabin playing poker. I'm supposed to bring him luck, but I had to get some air. Too smoky in there. He told me to get him a beer." She held the cup with both hands peeking out of Stinocher's jacket sleeves. "What's the name of this river?"

The river was twenty yards ahead of us. We wandered over to the bank, dew on the tall grass near the riverbank soaking through my sneakers.

"Wapsipinicon," I said. "Old-timers call it the Wapsi. You from around here?"

"Uh-uh. My father transferred here two years ago from Des Moines, and I decided I wanted to live with him. I couldn't stand my mother's boyfriends always hitting on me. My parents are divorced."

"That's terrible," I said.

She heaved a big sigh. "That's why I don't drink. I don't want to be a drunk like my mom." A moment's pause. "You live with just your father, don't you?"

I nodded.

"Your parents divorced?" she said.

"Nope."

I took a gulp of beer and realized I had an opportunity to become a hero in my own eyes by telling Bambi the truth about my mom, but I didn't. I told her The Lie. It was easier than telling the truth. I knew the story better. I had it rehearsed. It made me sound like a person in need of sympathy. But I spared Bambi the part about Mom's writing a letter explaining how much she loved me and was waiting for me in heaven.

Bambi must have thought I sounded choked up or

something, because she said, "I feel so sorry for you, but at least you had a mom who loved you."

"Yeah." I kicked at the grass and dirt at my feet. "I'm sure she loved me."

A sudden splash startled both of us. Bambi gave a little shriek and jumped closer to me. "What was that?"

"Carp," I said. "They work the shoreline in the spring at night."

"Scared the hell out of me," she said, and laughed. "I spilled some of Pete's beer."

"He's probably dying of thirst by now."

"He can wait. May I say something?"

"Sure."

Bambi looked up at me in the moonlight. "I watched you play football and basketball all year. Cheered at all your games. I thought you were terrific." She bent down and set Stinocher's beer by her feet in the grass. I finished mine off. "But you never once looked at me," she said. "Or talked to me."

I shook the last drops of beer out of my cup onto the ground. I was wearing a sweatshirt, and suddenly I was very warm.

I tried to choose my words carefully. "Look," I said. "Truthfully, I haven't had much time for girls. Sports and school and all. And I do a lot of stuff with my dad."

"Melody says you've got a thing for Angel McPherson."

I looked at the sky. The stars. The moon. "We've talked a few times."

"You know the rumor about her? She's gay."

"I don't listen much to rumors."

"Has she mentioned it?"

"No."

Bambi reached up and touched my cheeks with the

fingertips of both hands. My face was hot, and her fingers were ice cold from the cup of beer she'd been holding. "If the rumor turns out to be true, and she's not what you want, we could have lots of fun together. What's your sign?"

"Sign?"

"Astrological sign—when were you born?"

"February nineteenth."

"Pisces! We're a perfect match."

Her palms cupped my face. My head lowered. Bambi is much shorter than Angel. That didn't seem to make any difference, though. She raised up on her tiptoes, my lips fumbled for hers, and I kissed her. I don't know why. Kissed her right there on the riverbank in the moonlight, where someone wandering by could see us, her arms looping my neck as she kissed me back, her mouth hot and moist, smashing my lips, as I inhaled the flowery scent of her perfume.

She released me and stepped back, breathless, talking rapidly. "I'll take Stinocher his beer, I'll be right back." She picked the cup off the ground.

My heart was pounding so hard I thought it might beat its way out of my chest. "Bad idea," I said, and took a deep breath.

"We can find some place to be alone."

"Worse idea. A guy shouldn't mess with another guy's girl."

"Stay right here, I'll be back."

"I won't be here."

I watched Bambi skip away toward the cabin, my mouth dry. Hardly a drop of beer would be left in Stinocher's cup. His letter jacket was so long on Bambi, it covered her bottom, revealing her bare legs, making it look as if she weren't wearing cutoffs, as if her bottom were bare.

I needed to be doused with a bucket of cold water.

I crumbled my beer cup, tossed it into a trash barrel, and took off running for my Jeep.

12.

Sunday morning, Dad flipped the lights on in my room at 6:00 A.M., still dark outside, and said we were going wall-eye fishing in the Mississippi with a couple of his faculty buddies. They'd called yesterday while I was gone.

I bolted up in bed, startled and blinded by the light, then flopped my head back onto the pillow, eyes squeezed shut. A couple of years ago, I would have leaped out of bed, jumped into my clothes, and lugged all our fishing gear to the boat on the concrete slab in the backyard.

But this morning, I said, "Not me. Roasting a pig is hard work, I'm tired."

"What time did you get home?"

I'd taken a shower before I went to bed last night, but I could still smell my hog-smoky clothes in a pile on the floor.

"Before you did," I said. "Nine-thirty."

"Kids drinking beer there?"

I wrapped the warm pillow around my ears. "That's not why I'm tired, Dad. I had to do everything myself. Even clean up."

"Way it always is. I've told you that." I could still hear him through the pillow. "Going to be a nice day."

"Catch a five-pounder for me."

A long pause. Silence. More silence. I opened one eye. The room was dark. I fell back to sleep.

The phone woke me at eight o'clock. Running around the house looking for the cordless, rubbing my gritty eyes, I found it in the living room on the TV. I hauled the thing back into my room and collapsed on the bed. Tony.

"What happened to you last night? First thing I know, I look around, your Jeep and the cooker are gone."

"I ate, then drank a beer and got tired."

"Bambi Powers was going ape looking for you. She ran up to me by Spear's truck all excited and goes, 'Where's Danny? Where's Danny? Have you seen Danny?' The first thing I do is look for your Jeep and the cooker. They've vanished, and her face scrunches up like she's going to cry because she's so disappointed. What happened?"

"I don't know how it happened, man, but what happened is we ended up alone on the riverbank in the dark, and I kissed her."

I heard him chuckle. "She's something, isn't she?"

I gave him the details and said, "But I decided not to wait for her, she was with Stinocher."

"I can't believe it," he said. "Angel McPherson, Bambi Powers. I'm keeping Melody out of your reach."

"All girls do is mix a guy up."

"Look, call Bambi, apologize, tell her you got sick. Ask her if she'd like to do something today. You, me, Bambi, Melody—we'll hang out."

"Where?"

"I don't know, I haven't talked to Melody."

"I'd rather ask Angel."

A hefty silence. I could see him shaking his head. At

last he said, "Do what you've got to do. Whatever. Call me back, about noontime, let me know."

I made breakfast. Scrambled eggs, bacon, toast, jelly, milk. Ate and washed my dishes. I read the Sunday sports pages. Cubs lost again. Did my laundry. I managed to fool around until eleven before I called Angel, even though I knew I wasn't supposed to call.

I think her mother answered. Same whispery voice. "Hello."

I bit my bottom lip. "Is Angel home?"

"Why, yes. Just a moment, please, I'll get her."

A moment later. "Hello." Angel's voice, a tone softer than her mother's.

"Hi," I said. "Remember me? Danny Henderson."

"Hi."

"I thought I'd better call. Since I hadn't heard from you."

I hoped I didn't sound sarcastic. But I must have because to me, I sounded just like my dad.

"Danny, I'm sorry for waiting so long. I called yesterday—"

Sure you did.

"—and talked to your dad. He said you were busy and hung up."

Now I felt guilty.

I filled her in about Ricky Allen's birthday party on the Wapsi and my cooking my first pig by myself, ever. I didn't mention Bambi. I said, "I asked you to go, remember? But you didn't answer You didn't call, either."

Now she was silent again, but for only a few seconds. "Danny, I need to talk to you."

"Would you like to hang out this afternoon with me

and a couple of friends, Tony Gomez and Melody Reeves?
You might know them. Melody for sure."

"No, not with anybody else, I'd rather not."

"But you want to see me? Talk to me?"

"It's all right if you don't want to."

"I didn't say that." This girl had the potential to tick
me off. "I'll pick you up at your house."

Surprise! She said okay. Bring the basketball. We'd go
to the park again. She had some more advice for me about
my shooting. Pick her up at noon, she'd wait for me at the
curb.

I called Tony and explained what was happening.
"She's one weird chick," he said. "She didn't answer when
you asked her out. She doesn't want you to call. She gets
bent out of shape if you get too close to her house, and
now she doesn't want to go out with anyone else. Only
you. What do you make of it?"

"I don't know."

"She's gay, dumbshit."

"How does all of the above equal gay? Explain that!
She kissed me."

"Maybe she's not sure of her persuasion. She's using
you as an experiment."

"I don't believe it."

"Well, it's about time you find out what's going on."

"You're right about that."

"You don't want to pass up a morsel like Bambi Powers again."

"Right."

"Amen, buddy!" he sang out before hanging up.
"You've finally seen the light."

13.

I slid into a corner booth and sat across from Angel at Happy Joe Mooney's old-fashioned soda fountain/ice cream parlor—no video games, just a jukebox and gumball machines. The ceiling and walls are painted in wide red-and-white stripes, and the counter girls wear red-and-white striped blouses and skirts. No air-conditioning, either. Giant black fans hang from the ceiling, blades revolving slowly.

I clutched a triple-scoop black walnut ice cream cone in my right hand, a napkin in my left, while Angel gazed in amazement at her giant butterscotch sundae, crushed pecans and a cherry on top, all packed in a green cut-glass bowl.

"Heard about this place," Angel said, smiling, "but I've never been here before."

"Thought you'd like it. The cheerleaders and girls from the basketball team come here a lot after practice. You never go with them?" I aimed the question right at her.

Slight hesitation. No eye contact as Angel fiddled with her crutches so they fit next to her in the booth. "No, I haven't."

"You might be the only person in town who hasn't tasted Mooney's ice cream." I swiped my tongue across the top of my black walnut cone "You're in for a treat."

Angel scooped a spoonful of her sundae into her mouth, swallowed, smacked her lips, her gray eyes lighting up, and said, "Wow! This is so creamy."

"Mooney makes his own," I said. "I don't know how he does it."

We enjoyed our ice cream in silence a moment.

"Been working on your free throws?" Angel said.

I wondered when she was going to get to that. After our last session, I'd stuffed the progress charts she'd given me under the driver's seat in the Jeep and hadn't looked at them again until this noon when I piled into the Jeep to get her.

On one of the sheets, she'd rated me poor-to-fair in all categories, but at the bottom she'd drawn a smiley face, and underneath it she'd written, "Hang in there, Danny. I think you're cool. You can do it!"

I tried to avoid her gaze now by sucking a nut off the side of my second scoop of ice cream, and I stuck my nose into the top scoop.

Angel laughed and shoved one of her napkins across the table. She'd taken more than one. "You should eat your cone from the top. Works better."

"Thanks," I said, and wiped my nose, my mouth.

"So tell me," she said, "have you shot at least a hundred shots a day? Or more?"

"Not a one," I said, and avoided her gaze again by squishing my ice cream down into the cone with the flat of my tongue.

She rapped her spoon off the tabletop. "You said you were serious, Danny. Committed. You have to do this on your own, you know."

Not all on my own, I wanted to say, but didn't get the words out because the sight of a redhead at the counter with short curly hair, her back toward us, shook me. In white shorts and a blue tube top, from the rear view, she looked stacked like Bambi Powers. She held a little boy, his face over her left shoulder, who was sucking his thumb.

Angel caught me staring at them. "You know that girl?" she said. "I think I do."

"I'm not sure."

The clerk handed the redhead a chocolate cone, and when she turned, I gave a little start and froze. I was looking again into the smiling green eyes of Bambi Powers.

She could've ignored me, walked out with the kid, but she didn't. Bambi's smile grew wider as she said, "Hi, Danny."

I squirmed. "Hi."

I didn't call her by name, which, I hoped, indicated I didn't know her very well—I didn't. Only well enough to kiss.

She flicked a look at Angel sitting across from me and said, "Hi," then, holding the cone, she fed the little boy several licks of chocolate ice cream.

Angel said, "Hello."

Bambi eyed the crutches next to Angel. "Heard about your accident. What a crummy deal."

"Couldn't be helped."

"I guess everyone stops at Mooney's for ice cream," I said, hoping that if there had to be a conversation, I could steer it in the direction of meaningless banter.

"This is Tommy." Bambi smiled at the boy and shifted him in her arms. His brown hair hung over his ears and framed a round face with huge brown eyes. Three or four years old. "I baby-sit him. Made a mistake once and brought him here, now he wants to come all the time."

"He's cute," Angel said.

"Ice cream, please," the boy said, and reached for the cone.

"Knows what he wants," I said. "And polite."

Bambi fed him another lick, looked at me, and said, "I missed you last night. I came looking for you. What happened?"

I coughed. Sputtered. "I—I was tired and went home. I was supposed to get up early and go fishing with my dad."

She looked at me, head cocked. I felt ice cream dripping onto my hand. She must have been thinking, Then what are you doing here with her? Why aren't you fishing?

"I didn't get up in time," I said, and grabbed Angel's last napkin.

Bambi beamed another smile at me, as if Angel were nowhere in sight. "Well, I had a wonderful time. You were awesome." She shifted Tommy to her other arm. "Call me."

And with that, she turned and strutted out.

I felt limp. I wanted to slide under the table like my ice cream was sliding down my cone.

You were awesome.

"I can explain," I said to Angel. "The pig I cooked, that was *awesome*. That's what she meant."

"No need to explain anything," Angel said, and stabbed at the ice cream in the bottom of her green glass bowl.

We finished eating in silence. After we got outside in the hot sun and climbed into the Jeep, she said, "Did you bring the basketball?"

I bobbed my head yes, and said, "We can do something else if you like."

"I want to go to the park with you one more time."

"What's that mean, 'one more time'?"

Angel adjusted her crutches between us in the Jeep.

Didn't answer. I was being ignored again.

I hated that, but I let it drop.

The basketball courts at the park were full of kids playing. Picnickers, as far as I could see, sat at every table, eating, drinking, laughing, a smoking grill next to them. The softball diamonds were full and so were the tennis courts. What did I expect? It was a sunshiny Sunday afternoon after a couple of rainy days.

I found a place to park because I was lucky. Someone was pulling out as I was pulling in.

"Looks like we're sunk," I said, and shut down the Jeep. "We can sit under a tree or something. Talk."

Angel shook her head. "I think I can explain this right here." She shifted in her seat to face me. "Start shooting free throws from four, five feet away from the basket. Till you make them every time. Then back up a bit. Then a little bit more. Does that make sense?"

I nodded.

"Here's the big thing," she said. "Remember that feeling in your arm when you make them." She held her right hand up, flicked her wrist at my forehead as if it were a backboard, and extended her fingers as if she were shooting a basketball. "Remember the feel of the ball as it leaves your fingertips." She flicked her wrists again. "Try to duplicate that 'just-right' feeling every time. That's important."

"Sure.

"But you have to practice every day. That's more important." She cocked her head. "Practicing, why haven't you been practicing?"

"You want the truth?"

"Why not?"

I hit her with it. "I ask you to go out, you ignore me. You say you'll call, you don't. And you don't want me to call." I waved a hand. "I've been ticked off, that's why."

"Are you committed to playing better basketball or not? None of that should make any difference."

I hurled another chunk of honesty at her. "Our kissing turned me on. I thought maybe it did the same to you."

I waited for her to say something, but she only bit her bottom lip and closed her eyes a second.

"Well, maybe it didn't," I said, "but when I asked you for a date, I didn't expect to be ignored. I never expected that."

Swiveling in her seat, she faced the windshield. She puffed out a long breath and shook her head. "God!" she muttered. She grabbed her crutches lying between the seats, pushed open the door, slid out, and hippety-hopped around on one foot until she slipped the crutches under her armpits.

I scrambled out of the Jeep as she began striding away.

"Hey, where are you going?" I demanded.

My first thought was she was going to hit the bike path and head home. I knew she could do it on crutches, no problem.

But she halted and pointed a crutch out toward the park. "Meet me under that tree. I've got something to tell you," she said, and started marching toward a hundred-year-old oak fifty yards away.

She *is* gay!

14.

I hurried along behind Angel in the sunshine, biting my lower lip, knowing I was going to regret her revelation.

She wore a white cotton T-shirt and maroon shorts, her usual getup. She couldn't stuff her cast through a blue-jean leg. Maybe she didn't own a dress. Her thigh muscles rippled as she swung her crutches forward, stepped, swung them forward again, stepped.

She'd coiled her blond hair behind her head at the nape of her neck—that was different—and had tied the bun with a maroon ribbon to match her shorts.

When she arrived in the shade under the oak, she swung to face me, her face a little pink and sweaty. Cool air circulated under the tree's gnarled branches, but I felt sweaty, too, and wondered if my cheeks were also red. They felt like it.

"I should never have called you," Angel said, waggling her head. "Bad mistake. Big mistake."

"Why?" I jammed my hands deep into my jean pockets. "Give me one reason why."

"At the assembly, when you were shooting free throws, trying so, so hard, so awkward, I felt sorry for you. I did and—"

"Awkward!" I said, standing straight, squaring my shoulders. "I canned eighteen. Do you happen to recall that?"

"—and later you said you wished I'd teach you to shoot free throws, and then I called; I can't believe I did that. I tried to back out. I hung up. I knew something stu-

that. I tried to back out. I hung up. I knew something stupid like this would happen. . . ."

She kept babbling, rocking sideways a little on her crutches, looking at the ground, not meeting my eyes.

"I mean, I should've known we couldn't concentrate on just basketball. That's what I planned, just basketball."

"Look," I said, "tell me what's going on. Like why did you let me kiss you, then blow me off?"

She stopped, still looking at the ground, and dug at the grass with the tip of her right crutch. She flicked me a glance.

"Just come out and say it, will you, Angel?"

She said, "You are nice, Danny. The coolest guy."

I folded my arms across my chest. "That's wonderful to hear."

"You know how hard it is to not do something you want to do? How much willpower it takes? I shouldn't have let you kiss me, but I couldn't stop. I didn't try. I even told you to."

"Go out with me. You want me to beg, I'm begging."

"I don't want you to beg." She heaved a big sigh. "We can't see each other anymore, that's all I can say. We just can't, that's it, and you can do me a really, really big favor by not asking why. Or asking anything else."

"Have you ever dated anyone?"

"Grab Bambi Powers, she's crazy about you. I saw it in her eyes."

"Not interested."

"Work on your free throws." She clutched the handgrips on her crutches and steadied herself on her left leg. She cast her eye toward the bike path. She breathed once, deep. "I'm going home. This time I can make it myself."

I stepped in front of her.

"Please get out of my way."

I firmed my lips. Stiffened my stance. Didn't say anything. Refused to budge.

"I'll scream. This park is full of people."

I figured it was time to apply some full-court pressure.

"You're gay, aren't you?" That's the way it came out, point-blank like that. My eyes on her felt hard as stones.

She wobbled back three steps and bumped into the tree.

"But listen," I said. "Maybe you're not, maybe you just think you are. Maybe there's a chance for us."

Her face was perfectly white, like her shirt. "Who told you that? Who?" she demanded.

"Nobody." I sliced a hand through the air. "I've been figuring it out myself, okay?"

"Who?" She screamed it.

"I don't believe it, Angel. Listen to me—"

"Bambi Powers?"

"What difference does it make who? Is it true?"

"That means all the cheerleaders and my teammates think—Oh, fuck!"

"What do you expect? You act so . . . so different."

Her face crumpled. Tears exploded in her eyes. She lifted her hands to cover her face. Her crutches fell forward in slow motion. She sagged to the ground, the black bark on the oak tree clawing at the back of her T-shirt, pulling it up.

I tried to catch her crutches but was too late, and they fell into the grass.

I knelt in front of her.

Raising her knees, she pressed her forehead against them and wrapped her arms around her legs. I'd seen her cry before, but these sobs were worse than the physical pain of her broken ankle.

I felt helpless.

I sat back on my haunches and spread my arms out, as if to embrace Angel and the tree. "Hey, it's all right! I don't care! We'll work around it."

She kept rocking back and forth, but finally, she lifted her head to wipe her tears with the heel of her hand.

"I should've known," she muttered. "I'd never tried this before, but I should've known. Should've been able to figure it out."

"Tried what? You want to explain to me what's going on? If it's what I think it is, I already told you we'll make it work."

She hugged her knees again, but this time, threw her head back and looked straight up into the tree.

I couldn't help it. I said, "Careful. Lot of birds up there."

She looked at me and almost smiled. She said quietly, "I'm not gay, Danny. Far from it."

Music to my ears. "I knew it!"

She blew out a long breath through her teeth. "My mom and her friend Diane are gay, though."

I blinked. "Gay?"

I must've sounded as if I suddenly didn't understand the word.

"Lesbians," Angel said. "They've been together three years."

I bit my bottom lip and looked away.

"Sickening," she said, "right? Disgusting. My mom's a lesbo, what a freak I must be."

"I didn't say that."

"You can't even look at me."

I faced her. "Are you telling me the truth?"

"I knew that's how you'd react. It's how everyone re-acts. It's why I should've never—" She broke off. "Good-bye. I'm tired of going through this."

She started crawling on her hands and knees toward her crutches.

"You're not going anywhere," I said.

I grabbed her wrists, wrestled with her a moment, and pinned her on her back in the grass, holding her arms down on either side of her head, my body half across hers.

She gritted her teeth, her face turning red. "Tough football player! Picking on a crippled girl."

She tried to wrench her wrists free, but couldn't, her eyes brimming with tears.

"Diane's not your aunt?" I was breathing hard.

"She's my mom's fucking lover. Now let me up, Danny, so you can go yell it from the rooftops."

I released her and said, "Explain this to me, Angel. Please."

She pushed herself up and brushed off her arms.

"I'm not going to blab," I said.

"Yeah. Right. You know how kids treat you when they find out your mom's queer?"

"Angel, listen—"

"Try being a sixth grader and having your classmates laugh at you at recess because one of them saw your mom and her lover holding hands at the grocery store, and she told everyone. I mean, all of them laughing at you. And for the rest of the year, they smirk and giggle behind your back."

"I know, kids can be mean."

"Wait till your best friend gets mad and calls you a faggot and tells your secret to everyone else. That happened at my last high school." Angel shook her head. "My whole life, all I've wanted is just to be thought of as normal. I mean I don't even care if I am normal. Just if someone would think of me that way." She shuddered.

Now it was clear to me why Angel McPherson had no

friends at school, didn't date. Why she tried to keep me away from her house.

And now she was feeling frightened and helpless, sitting here in the grass under an oak tree with a broken ankle, crying, facing a two-hundred-thirty-pound bully. Hadn't I just wrestled her onto her back? And she couldn't storm off because her crutches were behind me, out of her reach. Worse, I'd blown her cover. I'd discovered her secret. Her lie.

I stood up and gathered her crutches off the ground. I held my hand down to her. She grabbed it, without looking at me, and I pulled her to her feet. That was a move I was getting good at. I nestled one crutch under her left arm, and she took the other one from me.

We didn't say anything.

Somehow I had to convince her I didn't care about her mom and Aunt Diane and that I was good at keeping secrets.

I expected Angel to march off toward the bike path and head home. I'd go with her, at least to the point where she had to leave the path to get to her house, but she aimed herself toward the tree, got there in half a dozen steps, turned, and leaned against it.

"I don't want to leave you with the wrong impression," Angel said.

The coil of hair at the nape of her neck was coming loose. Wrestling had messed it up. She pulled out the maroon ribbon, then spread her fingers wide and ran them through her hair, which fell to her shoulders.

"I love my mother," Angel said. "Lesbo, queer, faggot—I never think of her like that. I just wanted you to understand what other people think. Maybe you think the same way. Nearly everybody else does. But I love her."

"We've got a gay guy on the football team. I don't

92

care. He's a tough defensive tackle, that's what matters. I don't even think my dad knows."

"My mom's an incredibly brave and strong person. She has to be, being in real estate, being who she is. Life's not easy for her."

"You know what I think?"

Angel wasn't listening. "My mom's everything to me, but it's so difficult to explain her, and I want so bad to get away from her, it nearly kills me with guilt."

"Look, Angel, what's obvious here is, your mother, your aunt—none of it makes any difference to me."

"She's not my aunt. She's my mom's third lover, since I can remember."

Angel rubbed her eyes with the heel of her hand. "I thought I could get through high school here, keeping my little secret this time, then I'd be off to college thousands of miles away from my mom and Diane, playing basketball, but I've failed."

"I'm not going to tell anyone, Angel."

"Until you get mad at me and want to get even for something. Then you'll tell the world. I know, I've been through it before."

Her nose was red, her bottom lip quivered, but her eyes were almost dry now.

Five or six little kids came scrambling by, yelling, screaming, kicking a soccer ball. Two of them collided, tumbled over, got up, and raced after the others, the kicker way in front.

"I've got an idea," I said.

"I just want you to understand how I feel about my mother. I love her. She's a good person; so is Diane. Make sure you tell that to everyone." Angel gathered her crutches under her arms. "I'm going home now. You don't have to take me this time."

"Not yet."

"Get out of my way." She waved me aside with a crutch. "Please!"

I moved and allowed her to get one step beyond me, then said, "You and I, Angel McPherson and Danny Henderson, we squelch all rumors at school about your being gay by becoming a couple. We make out in my Jeep in the morning before school. We hold hands and walk each other to class. We kiss in front of our lockers."

Suddenly Dad's angry face loomed in my mind. I pictured him standing over Angel and me in front of my locker. Fuming. But I zapped the picture. I'd deal with him later. Not now.

Angel stopped and twirled around. "You are so full of it, Danny."

"I'm serious. We steam up the school. We go to a school dance. Get kicked out because we can't keep our hands off each other. They find us in my dad's SUV in the parking lot, half our clothes off—"

"You're crazy!"

"—and now who says Angel McPherson is gay? Because everyone's tongue at school is wagging about how hot we are together."

I ambled over to her in the sunshine. We turned, and I let her pick the way, the bike path or my Jeep, both in the same general direction, but eventually she'd have to veer one way or the other.

We scuffed along in the grass. Dandelions were beginning to pop their golden heads, just today.

"You're crazy," Angel said. "I didn't think you were so crazy."

"Making me a good free-throw shooter, is that a crazy idea? No! Neither is this one."

She looked away.

"Does your mom care if you date boys? Does she want you to be—" I didn't know how to say it.

"Like her?" Angel shook her head. "She begs me to date."

"I'm your man," I said, beaming.

Angel kept shaking her head, as if everything I was suggesting really was crazy. "You think you don't care, Danny, but I promise you, if word ever got out about my mom, you have no idea how cruel people can be. If you were dating me, you'd be laughed out of school. Probably your dad, too."

"Who's going to tell?"

We'd reached the edge of the parking lot. Angel had to make a choice. She didn't hesitate. She angled toward my Jeep.

Yes!

"I've never hung out with a guy before," she said. "Not seriously."

"You don't hang with anyone," I pointed out.

"Not here, but I used to." She huffed out a breath. "I just thought we'd mess around a little with basketball. I never thought—it was stupid of me."

I drove her home. On the way, she said, "Why don't you already have a girlfriend?"

"Too ugly," I said. "And my dad keeps me busy."

I parked in front of her house and walked her to the door.

"Do we have a deal?" I kissed her right there on her front porch for the whole rest of the world to see. A tiny kiss.

She didn't seem surprised. Didn't fight it. Kissed me back.

I said, "Your mom and Aunt Diane are gone, aren't they? That's why we can kiss on your front porch."

"Yes, both of them."

"Won't the neighbors tell?"

"They don't associate with us."

"Deal?" I said again. "We make out like crazy at school. Go to a couple of school things—the All-School Talent Show—and paw each other till the teachers yell at us."

"I don't know," she said. "I've got to think."

"What's to think about? Call me tonight, okay?"

She shook her head. "Later, I'll be in touch. Not tonight. Go practice your free throws." She gave me another little kiss and disappeared inside the house.

I sighed. I knew I had a chance with her, and that thought sent me bounding down the walk to my Jeep. But I also knew that, not only would Dad dislike the fact I'd gotten myself interested in a girl, but he would also hate the fact that her mom was gay and lived with a lover. I could hear him yelling at me, "She's a *what?*"

Suck it up, Dad. It's time I live my own life.

I climbed into the Jeep. Started it.

Maybe I didn't need to tell him about Angel's mom. Just like he'd kept my mom's secret from me.

15.

Two days after Angel and I had kissed on her front porch, we met after school at the picnic table in the park where we'd shared our first kiss. Another cloudy day.

She arrived on her crutches and sat across from me.

"I want to see you, Danny," she announced.

Yes! Beautiful!

"But only if we keep our meetings secret. No one can know. No one at school. Not your dad, my mom. Nobody."

My eyebrows raised. "Didn't you tell me your mom wants you to have a boyfriend?"

"Yes, she does. So does Diane."

"Then why hide from them? Let's tell them."

"My mom would smother us. She'd want to invite you over all the time. Like for dinner. Eventually you'd have to explain her to your dad. He'd tell somebody, even though he might say he wouldn't."

"We can't hide forever. We're bound to run into people accidentally, like we did Bambi Powers."

"Danny, I don't want people asking questions about me, digging. I've been through this, I keep telling you. Soon everybody knows your business. What they don't know, they make up, and that's worse."

"So we have to hide?"

"Yes. Nothing's going to change. Not my mom, Diane. Nothing. I can't do anything about them."

"Ashamed of who you are?"

I reached across the table and held her hands.

Her cheeks turned pink.

"Afraid?" I said.

"I know how it feels to be rejected. Lied about. The fewer people I'm close to, the fewer people who know me, the better."

"What about our basketball plans?"

She looked away the moment our eyes might have met. "You're going to have to work out most of the time alone."

I let it go. I was so thrilled she'd see me I didn't protest anymore. Shows you how weak I was. How much

I wanted her. One good point about Angel's game plan: I wouldn't have to explain her to my dad. But how long could a relationship built on secrets and lies last?

What Angel and I would do, most nights, was meet after dark in the Duck Creek parking lot, and take off together in my Jeep for an hour or so, never much longer. I didn't have any problem slipping out of the house for a short time. Tony was my excuse, though he didn't know it. For Angel, getting away was tougher. Her excuse was that she was jogging on her crutches on the bike path as best she could, trying to keep up her stamina for when she got her cast off and returned to basketball. She went at night because there were fewer people, and since streetlights lit the path, she felt safe. Her mom bought the lie because I never kept Angel out very long, and Angel's jog on her crutches from the park to her house, after I'd dropped her off, was enough to work up a believable little sweat.

We went to different spots and parked, depending on how alone we figured we could be, and at the same time, how safe we were. The first night of our romance, we drove to Look-Out Point, a scenic spot overlooking the Mississippi River, where I knew guys parked with their girls to make out, but it was way too crowded. Someone was bound to recognize my Jeep, or us, so we ended up back in the parking lot at Duck Creek, which was now deserted. No one to see us hugging, kissing, panting. Lots of times, we drove out to Allen's Grove on the Wapsi River and parked in the tree-lined lane in the dark, unable to see the moon or stars, leaves rustling in the breeze. Once in a while, a screech owl scolded us. But Allen's Grove was a fifteen-mile drive each way and cut into our time together.

Were all girls like this? I wondered. Had I lucked out? Was Angel thinking and feeling the same way about me? And I was curious about her mom and dad. What was their life like together?

One night, as soon as we parked at Allen's Grove, Angel snuggled into my arms and I said, "Did your dad know your mom was gay? I mean, like was he still alive when she . . . you know, turned to a woman? Did they divorce?"

My questions seemed to confuse Angel. Only a bit of ghostly moonlight filtered through the tress, so I couldn't see her face, couldn't see if she was frowning or what. Maybe the questions were too personal. Finally, she said, "He didn't know. She didn't start that till after the crash and he was dead. She was lonely."

I thought about that. Maybe she already had a lesbian lover on the side, and he didn't know. But I didn't mention that to Angel.

"Too bad he had to die," I said. "They probably would've stayed together, and maybe we wouldn't be hiding now."

With her head lowered, she said, "Yes. Too bad."

"Or if he was alive and they were divorced, you'd at least have somebody to talk to about this. Or you could be living with your dad. That might be better."

Her warm fingertips touched my cheek. "Aren't you going to kiss me back?"

"You're lucky, you know. You have memories of your dad. I don't have any memories of my mom at all. I mean, I'm not asking you to feel sorry for me, I just want you to know how lucky you are."

"You're going to be unlucky if you don't kiss me."

I did as commanded.

That night, when I let Angel out of the Jeep in the park—I always got out to help her—she took two strides across the lot in the moonlight, then stopped.

She turned. I was standing near the Jeep's front fender.

"Hey, Danny," she called in her whispery voice. "I think I love you." And then she was gone.

I stood there dumbfounded. No girl had ever said she loved me. No one had ever said it. My dad had never said it, though I'm sure he did love me. Maybe if I'd had a mom who'd told me she loved me and had hugged and kissed me all the time, I would have burst out, "I love you, too, Angel McPherson." But I didn't.

Somehow after that night, the grass, trees, flowers, sky seemed more beautiful. Some days I felt as if I could float. Nothing bothered me. Not even my dad.

One sunny morning, as Tony and I sat in his truck before school, he said to me, "What's going on with you? All shiny-faced, smiling. You look like you're keeping the most awesome secret in the world. You connect with Angel? Bambi, maybe?"

"Just happy. It's near the end of the school year," I said, but I longed to tell him the truth.

That same long-to-tell-the-truth feeling gripped me when Bambi came bustling by my locker one afternoon in school, stopped, and smiled. "Been waiting for your call," she said. "Don't see you hanging with the Stone Angel."

"Busy," I said. If she only knew!

"Stinocher's out of the picture. Call me."

I shrugged. Weak smile. "Sorry."

"I'm waiting." Bambi skipped off.

At home, my improved attitude impressed even my dad when he found one evening that I'd washed my Jeep and his Expedition.

100

"What the hell's got into you?" he said, admiring both of the vehicles as they sat in the drive, gleaming in the late-afternoon sun.

"Nothing. They both looked dirty."

He shook his head. "Amazing."

Later, I slipped away into the darkness to be with Angel, keeping my secret.

That was the first time Angel revealed more about herself. We'd been talking about how life had been for us as kids, her without a dad, me without a mom. I told her I'd never had to worry about my dad's bringing a female home because he detested them.

Angel gave a wry laugh in the darkness of the Jeep, and said, "That's what I worried about all the time, my mom bringing home a female."

I didn't know if I should laugh or not—I thought it was funny. I gave a muffled chuckle. Then we both laughed out loud. Little by little, Angel told me bits of her life story before she arrived in Iowa. Like before she started school, she never felt ashamed about her situation with her mom and her "aunt." They only hung with people who accepted them, mainly other gays and lesbians. But once she started school, Angel couldn't escape the ridicule when people found out, so she lied a lot, especially so she could get invited to friends' houses and birthday parties. She invited friends to her house, but not before she got her mom and aunt to lie.

"I used to get totally mad at my mom, demanding to know why she chose to be this way, which made me so goddamned odd. Mom said she couldn't help the way she was, and then I'd regret having asked because I knew I'd hurt her."

I thought about telling Angel my little secret about my mom. But I didn't want her to stop talking about herself, and I didn't want her to think I was a wait-until-you-hear-my-story kind of guy. Listen to me, I can top that. Which I couldn't. Anyway, I felt there'd be plenty of time to unpack my baggage later.

Angel said the first aunt she could remember was Susan, and as a little girl, she had liked the woman. Susan played with her and read to her all the time. But Susan vanished from Angel's life when Angel was ten. Her mom said she and Susan had "grown apart."

A few years later came Linda. Angel was older now, knew what was going on between them, and fought night and day to get rid of her new aunt. "I told her I hated the meals she cooked, wouldn't wear the clothes she picked out for me, or accept any presents, like at Christmas or for my birthday. I wouldn't ride to school with her or let her pick me up. I was terrible. Linda lasted two years.

"One night, I heard Mom and her arguing in their room and Linda yelled, 'I can't stand your brat any longer! I'm out of here.' Mom yelled at her to leave now! Linda packed and left the next day, and my mom cried every night in her room for a week. But she never blamed me for losing her friend. I hurt so bad for my mom I decided not to interfere anymore."

The secret of my mom paled compared to the secrets Angel was lugging around. Angel had been so honest with me that it was obvious if I had an ounce of integrity, I'd have to tell her about my mom. I was sick of The Lie, anyway. By now, I should be grown up enough to deal with facts. Not hide them.

Time for the truth. But when? How? It's not easy to admit to someone you care for you've been a liar all this time. It's humiliating to admit you're weak and you haven't been man enough to face the truth. That you're a fraud.

Angel's and my torrid romance—I like that word, *torrid;* it's the right one—had gone on for three weeks when I decided to practice telling the truth about The Lie.

16.

"You want to hear something about me I've never told anyone else before?" I said. I cast my worm-baited treble hook into the muddy waters of the Wapsi River.

"You got herpes?" Tony said.

I shook my head. "Very funny."

I sat down next to him on the river's grassy bank. Sunday, 7:30 A.M. Another blue-sky morning. Thirty yards upriver is where I'd kissed Bambi Powers. Seemed like a long time ago. Thirty yards down the lane behind me is where I was currently making out with Angel McPherson.

Tony and I'd been fishing here before. We usually fished until about one or two, when it got too hot. Ricky Allen's folks didn't care, as long as we picked up our garbage and hauled it with us, which we always did. In past years, we'd caught some nice catfish, five- and six-pounders.

"I'm serious," I said. "I've got something I need to tell you."

Tony is the first person at Big River High that I'd lied to. When I was a kid, everyone back in Saginaw had known about my mom for a long time, except me, until I forced the truth out of my dad when I was twelve. My cousin Lynette, my mother's sister's daughter, was a real snotty know-it-all. We were in the same class, but my dad didn't want me to hang with her because he hated her mother.

Lynette had just proven me wrong in math class about how many feet are in a mile, and I was still arguing with her at recess time on the playground. I said, "You don't know half as much as you think you do."

"I know more than you do!" she shot back, red-faced. "I know your mom didn't die of cancer. She died in a motorcycle accident on the back of her boyfriend's bike. Slut!"

I would rather have been punched out by the school's biggest bully, Jimmy Freeman. I felt like I had been.

That night after school, I tried not to cry when I asked my dad about it. After a lot of hemming and hawing and a couple of big hugs, he said, "Yes, Danny, it's true."

I was dumbstruck. And I was mad at him.

"Why did you lie to me?" I demanded.

He said he wanted to protect me from the truth. He wanted me to have a good picture of Mom in my mind when I was young. He said a boy needed that. He said he'd always planned to tell me the truth when I was old enough and he thought I could handle it.

I didn't talk to him for a week. And that's when I wrote my second letter to Mom.

As I got older, I began to think there were other reasons for his lying to me. Like he wanted to protect himself, too. He was embarrassed that his wife took a lover, which diminished his manliness.

I felt ashamed, too. I hadn't had a mother who loved me enough to be faithful to my dad and keep us together as a family. When Dad and I moved to Big River, and Tony and I became friends, I lied to him. Lying about Mom seemed normal. Dad had lied to me.

Tony said, "Something you need to tell me, huh? Let's see." He scratched his head. "You and the Stone Angel have been doing it every night. She likes it." He wiggled his pole. Reeled in some line.

I shook my head, bit my bottom lip.

"Listen to me," I said. "You remember the first time we met, in seventh-period gym class, and the coach was there and asked if we'd like to go out for basketball? I was the new kid."

"You were the biggest, clumsiest nerd I'd ever seen."

"I told you a lie after school."

"What lie? Did I see you after school?"

"We walked home together, you gave me half your Milky Way, and I told you a lie."

I retold the lie about Mom's cancer to refresh his memory. And then, looking at the river rolling by, I told him the truth about my mom, a lump in my throat all the time. "My mom had a lover, a biker guy. My aunt—my mom's sister—let them use her house to meet. One time, my mom was on the back of the guy's bike, and he had an accident. He ran into the back of a truck. Both of them were killed. They'd been out drinking." I hung my head. Let out a giant breath. "I wasn't even a year old. That's it. That's all I know."

The relief I felt was immediate.

We were silent a moment, watching the tip of Tony's pole nod once, twice, three times.

"Might be a carp," Tony said. "Catfish are hitting harder than that."

We'd already caught three nice catfish, three-pounders, at least, and had them on a stringer, but Tony's pole was still now.

"A carp," I said, and heard a woodpecker tap-tap-tapping hell out of a tree behind us in the woods.

Tony nodded. "Thought you were keeping a secret,

the way you been acting lately, like the world's a wonderful place. But what I thought was maybe you're banging Angel. Bambi even. Maybe both of them. And you were afraid to tell anybody because they told you not to. Made you promise. That's how Melody is."

Man, I wanted so bad to tell him I was seeing Angel, but I couldn't betray her. He'd tell Melody. She'd stand in front of school and blab it. Angel would hate me forever.

"So what's the point?" Tony said. "Why you telling me this?"

I reeled my line in, inspected my worm, still there, and cast out again. "When I was a kid, my dad told me that lie, and I told it to everyone else. It's time I grew up. Told the truth. Faced reality. However you want to say it."

"My grandparents were illegals from Mexico City. They worked for nothing in a meat-packing plant in Dubuque. Like slaves. I never lied about it, though. I just never told anyone. So now you know."

"You probably think I'm a jerk for lying to you."

"I've always thought you were a jerk." He gave me his white-toothed grin. "Now I kind of admire you, but not much. Don't let it go to your head, buddy."

"Thanks." I felt pretty good. Like a weight had been lifted from my shoulders.

Tony's pole took a sudden dive. "See that!" He held on with both hands and jumped up.

"You going to catch that fish or not?" I said.

I had launched my eighty-eighth free throw at the basket above our garage, when Dad came home from golfing about six o'clock. I'd hit fifty-three shots, better than fifty percent, but not good. From the street, he opened the garage door with the automatic door opener but parked in the drive. He lumbered out of his Expedition, leaving his clubs inside the vehicle.

He said, "You should've been with us, beautiful day at Emeis."

"Beautiful day fishing on the Wapsi. What did you shoot?"

"First liar doesn't stand a chance. How many fish you catch?"

I hit a baseline jumper. He picked up the ball and tossed in a layup.

I said, "I can prove how many fish we caught. Got 'em in the house, ready for supper tonight. You shoot in the eighties?"

He put up a little jumper, hardly got off his feet. Missed. I grabbed the loose ball. I noticed lately his belt seemed to be disappearing under his belly.

"Eighties?" I repeated.

"Hell, yes."

"Eighty what?"

"None of your business." He looked sheepish. "Eighty-nine."

I fired up an air ball from the corner and shook my head. Dad snared the rebound and held the ball. "Why don't you give this up?"

I shrugged. "I kind of like it. Haven't you always told me to be the best I can at whatever I try?"

Keeping the ball tucked in his arm, he walked into the garage. I followed. He said, "I'm starved. Let's see how many fish you got, I'll fry them up quick."

Tony and I had caught six nice catfish, Tony four of them, but he never took fish home. No one ate fish at his house. Dad deep-fried them to a golden brown in an electric skillet on our picnic table on the patio, while I fried up some frozen hash browns in the house on the stove and whipped up a cornbread mix from a box. I always wondered if Mom had been a good cook and would have made something like this from scratch.

We ate outside on the picnic table under the shade of our maple tree. Dad was in a good mood. The end of the school year was in sight. He'd played well today, for him. The fish was delicious. You can't beat fish that go straight from the water into the frying pan without being frozen.

I'd never find a better opportunity to talk to him. I waited until he took his last bite of fish and washed it away with a swig of beer.

I set my fork down, wiped my lips with a paper napkin, a lump in my throat again, and said, "I need to tell you something."

I must have sounded nervous. He gave me a quick glance and said, "You're not failing anything, are you? Now's not the time to tell me that, near the end of the semester." He took another swallow of beer. "Couldn't be that. Your counselor would've told me."

"It's not that. It's—"

Now one eyebrow slid up, and he eyed me hard. "Speeding ticket? Beer in the Jeep?"

He was always worried about beer because some of his football players had been caught drinking and driving.

"Nothing like that," I said.

"What?"

I took the plunge. "I've been going out with Angel McPherson."

The announcement blindsided him. His eyes got big, then narrowed. The thing about Dad is, he always starts out calm, but sometimes he can work himself up, depending on the situation.

He dropped his fork on his plate with a clatter and shoved the plate back. "Angel McPherson. I told you to leave her alone. Why don't kids listen these days? Jesus."

"Would you like any female I liked?"

That left him silent a moment, debating. The catfish and beer had made him sweat a little, beads on his forehead.

"I'll tell you something," he finally said. "You're seventeen, I realize that. I never figured I'd keep you away from females forever, but I've always hoped when you started I'd be able to talk you out of doing something foolish."

"What's foolish about Angel?"

"Find a different girl, have some fun if you have to, but—" He shifted his weight, and the picnic table creaked. "At your age, females are good recreation, Chief, no denying that, but—"

"But drop Angel," I said. "Is that what you're saying?"

"What do you know about her?"

"A lot."

He drilled me with a dark-eyed look. "Her mother's a lesbian and lives with a dyke. She tell you that?"

Now it was my turn to be blindsided. I nearly fell backward off the picnic table.

"How do you know?"

"Dunlap sells real estate part time. He and Angel's mother work out of the same office. He knows."

Angel's secret wasn't as well kept as she thought. She had no idea. This was terrible.

"Angel told me," I said. "But her mom and Diane, they don't make Angel gay, too, you know."

"No, but it might put her in contact with a lot of weirdo fags and their lifestyle, which I'd rather not have you be a part of."

"I've been to their house. They live like regular people."

"You have no idea how females can cause you to lose sight of your goals. Just turn your whole life upside down. I hate to see you go through that, but I guess you'll have to."

Dad swung his legs over the picnic table seat and stood up. His face was red. He wiped the sweat off his forehead with his palm.

"You caught and cleaned the fish," he said. "I'll take care of the dishes. We'll talk about this again, later."

He let it drop. I couldn't believe it. This was some kind of trick. Some new phase of child psychology he was using on me. He hadn't blown his cool or anything. He'd stopped before he got too worked up.

I ducked around to the front of the house and shot more baskets. I don't know how many. Two hundred, maybe. I didn't keep track of my percentage. Near dark, I'd figured it out. Dad was using the oldest trick in the world. He was going to let me stick my finger in the fire. Burn myself good. Then I'd never mess with fire again.

When I was a kid, maybe twelve, we were fishing and I caught a snapping turtle no bigger than the lid of a pickle jar. I got the hook out of its bottom lip and set the turtle next to me on the boat seat. It just sat there, all hunkered inside itself. "Don't think about playing with that," Dad said. "It's a snapper. He'll get you. Throw it back in."

"It's not doing anything."

"You'll see."

The turtle must have sat there five minutes, not moving. When dad wasn't looking, I stuck my finger down by its nose, teasing it. In an instant, it snapped the end of my finger and hung on. I shrieked, jumped up, and whipped my hand over the water. "Get it off!" I screamed. "Get it off!" The turtle flew off—but with a chunk of my finger in its mouth. Worse than that, when I'd bolted up, my pole flipped into the lake and sank. We never got it back. Dad was pissed. I thought he might throw me overboard to fish the rod and reel off the bottom of the lake. I never played with a snapper again.

Dad was in the basement, I knew. He often went down there to drink another beer, smoke a cigar, and watch TV after a meal he particularly liked.

I tromped down the steps. We had finished off the basement: drop ceiling, carpeting, couch, chairs, floor lamps, wet bar, pool table, fireplace. TV. Everywhere you looked a bass or a muskie hung on the wall, a deer head or a rack, a pheasant, or a turkey fan.

The basement smelled of cigar smoke. Dad slouched in his recliner, feet up, watching a fishing show he'd taped. Come fall, he'd be watching game films. Me, too. I drifted over to the bar and slid onto a stool.

The light from the TV screen and an Old Style beer sign spread a soft glow in the room and across the bar's polished wood.

"All the teachers at school know about Angel's mother and her friend?" I said.

He looked up from the TV. "Might, but I doubt it. It's not something they'd tell the kids, though." His stub of a cigar sat in an ashtray next to his beer on an end table. He reached for the cigar, flicked off the white ash, took a puff, blew out a cloud of smoke. "I'm sure Lee would like to keep her star focused on basketball. Can't you see how you've already complicated her life, breaking her ankle?"

He had a point.

"Let me ask you something," he said. "How come you told me about her?"

I leaned an elbow on the bar, trying to relax.

"I've been sneaking around with her. I'm getting tired of that. And I figured I should tell you before someone else did."

He nodded. "Good idea. Serious about her?"

"I like her a lot."

"If you have to sneak around behind my back, something must be wrong. Ever think of that, Chief?"

"Yes, but maybe we won't be sneaking around anymore."

He reached for his can of beer, realized it was empty, and set it back down. He puffed on his cigar instead, big rolling clouds this time, the tip glowing red as he squinted through the smoke.

"I won't tell you you can't see her," he said. "My folks told me that about your mom. 'You can't date her, you can't!' is all they ever said to me. It never worked."

"Why didn't they like her?"

He shrugged. "She had a reputation, and she lived up to it. She was in Max Fowler's bed right after you were born." He halted. Glanced at me, the colored light from the TV, mostly blue, reflecting off his face and head. I don't think he intended that last part to slip out. I'd never heard that man's name before.

"At seventeen," I pointed out, "I should get to pick my own friends."

He nodded. "I hope you'll be smart enough to realize this one's not good for you."

"Bet you'd like to have an athlete like her on your football team, say at quarterback."

He sank deeper into his chair, not answering that, and returned his cigar to the ashtray.

He wasn't going to change his mind about her.

I said, "So you think just a few teachers know about her mom and partner?"

"Far as I know. Why?"

"She's trying hard to hide it."

"Tough thing for a kid to handle. Other kids find out, they can be ferocious. Worse than sharks. That's why teachers keep their mouths shut about that stuff."

He turned back to the TV.

"I might be a little late tonight," I said. "I've got my homework finished. Don't worry about me."

"So that's where you've been going at night, to be with her?"

"Sometimes."

"Have I ever told you that the fewer females—"

"Don't even think it, Dad!"

That's when he shocked me again. "Bring her around here," he said. "I'd like to get a closer look."

"All right, I will."

That was about the best conversation I'd ever had with my dad, and I'd been honest all the way. But I knew he figured disaster loomed ahead for me.

17.

I'd planned an after-dark bonfire for Angel and me, something different from making out every night, getting all hot and aroused, breathing hard, then having to shut down before we really went too far. For a place, I picked the Atalissa limestone quarry abandoned by the Dewey Portland Cement Company maybe half a century ago, all surrounded by trees now, at the end of a dirt lane. Most kids don't know about it, just fishermen, so Angel and I had a good chance of being alone.

I'd snatched kindling and hunks of split-oak firewood

from home and stacked them in the back of the Jeep, along with a small cooler containing a big bag of marshmallows and four cans of Mountain Dew. Just after dark, Angel and I parked at the quarry's edge. Ten feet below, the water, covering an area bigger than a city block, rippled in the early moonlight. Lots of bass, crappie, and blue gill swim in that deep quarry water.

I lugged the wood out of the Jeep, stacked the kindling like a teepee around crumpled newspaper, lit it with a match, and gradually added hunks of oak. Finally the fire took off, and we sat cross-legged on the limestone bluff, Indian style, mesmerized in front of its crackling flames.

I'd thought of having Tony and Melody meet us here. Say about nine o'clock, they'd come strolling over to the fire and pretend we'd all met accidentally, and Angel would get to know someone else at school besides me. She'd realize Tony and Melody thought of her as an okay person. And so would everyone else at school. But I couldn't betray Angel again. I'd already told my dad I was seeing her, and I'd promised to tell no one.

We roasted the marshmallows on long sticks that I cut from a willow near the water's edge, and then drank the ice-cold Mountain Dew. Some of the marshmallows caught fire, got black and smoky, but we ate them anyway, and then kissed each other's sticky-sweet lips.

"Beautiful night," Angel said, leaning back on her hands, looking straight up at the sky, moon, and stars. We'd finished our last cans of pop and were full to our ears with marshmallows. "I'd like to stay here forever."

"Too bad we don't have sleeping bags."

"One would do," she said, smiling in the firelight.

"Want to skinny dip? Water's deep and cold."

"I have to go home, I'm going to be late. My mom will be suspicious."

"One little dip?"

"I can't go swimming with a cast on, anyway, silly."

I gathered up our empty cans in front of us, set them near the cooler. I cleared my throat. "I need to tell you something before we go. You've been so honest with me, I have to be honest with you."

She stared into the fire, still seated cross-legged, forearms resting on her bare thighs, waiting for me to go on.

"I lied about my mom," I said, then told her the true story, even about how I found out. "I just felt I should tell you," I said at the end. "I'm sorry I lied. I wanted you to think I had this cool family, a loving mom and dad, but I don't. Never did."

"I've lied to so many people about my mom," Angel said.

"I'm glad you trusted me enough to tell me the truth."

She looked away.

"Prom's Saturday night," I said. "I'm not much of a prom-goer, but I'd go with you."

She shook her head.

"Let's you and me kill this secret we've been keeping. Admit the truth to everyone. We're dating."

She shook her head again.

"You're due for a walking cast. I don't know how to dance, but I'd be willing to try at the prom, if you are."

She bit her bottom lip, angles in her face turning sharp in the firelight. "I can't."

"We should be having lots of fun. Carnival's in town first week of June. Want to go fishing? My dad has a boat."

"Let's go home, Danny. I'm late."

"We can't spend all of our time making out. We'll get sick of each other. Or something worse will happen."

"If you're sick of me, that's fine." Flatly.

"I didn't say that! Don't you want a real relationship?"

"Has ours been that terrible? I wasn't aware of that."

Angel grabbed her crutches and hoisted herself up. The Jeep was five steps away. We were leaving. "Got to put out the fire," I said, aware that if I pursued this further, I might put out the fire between Angel and me. I thought of Tony, always giving in to Melody. Now I understood him better.

I got up, grabbed the cooler, and splashed most of the ice water on the fire, its flames hissing and sputtering, going up in smoke. I kicked around the embers, a few sparks flying, and put them out with the last dose of water.

Angel had already climbed into the Jeep. Closed the door.

I loaded the cooler into the back of the Jeep and slid in next to her, in the driver's seat. I sat a moment with my hands clutching the steering wheel. "I thought maybe it was a good idea, honesty. I mean, I'm not an honesty freak. Don't get me wrong."

She didn't answer. I started the Jeep, pulled on the lights, whipped the thing around, and headed down the dirt lane that snaked through timber to a gravel road, fields of newly planted corn on either side.

What was going to happen now?

I thought maybe Angel wasn't going to say another word all the way home, but when we crunched to a halt on the gravel and I made the turn onto blacktop, she said, "In sixth grade, when I lived in Florida, we had our class picnic at a county park. There was a lake and a beach. We roasted hot dogs and marshmallows, like tonight. Four of us girls went together to the restroom. It was kind of far away in a grove of palms. On the way back, one of the girls spotted two women seated on a park bench making out. Kissing. Arms wrapped around each other. Kissing, big time.

"Everyone giggled. Except me. We hid between trees and watched. I wanted to run back to where the other girls were playing softball. I'd seen my mother kiss her girlfriends lots of times. I'd heard them make out in their bedroom. Linda was a screamer. You know what a screamer is?"

I shook my head. A deer sprinted thirty yards ahead of us across the road in the glare of the Jeep's headlights.

"Look at that!" I said.

But Angel went on as if the deer had never been in our sight.

"Anyway, the women discovered they were being watched. They heard us kids laughing—I didn't laugh. This wasn't funny to me. The women got up and left, holding hands.

"The four of us gathered under a tree. 'Dirty lesbians,' Ella said. 'Disgusting! My mom says they shouldn't be allowed in city parks.' 'Perverts!' Claudia said. 'My dad says all the lesbos and fags should be rounded up and shot!' That was my mom they were talking about. Shoot her! 'The worst thing,' June said, 'is you can't always tell who they are. I think I had one for a teacher. I didn't want her to touch me.' I didn't say anything. I was blushing so bad and hurt so bad, tears in my eyes, I turned and pretended the breeze had blown sand in my face. Then I ran away. I never looked any one of those girls in the eye again all through school. Never talked to them."

I was quiet. I didn't know what to say.

We were almost in the city now. The Jeep hummed

along. Another five minutes and we'd be home. It was ten o'clock. Angel was definitely late. My fault.

"What do you think those girls would've said to me if I'd told them the truth, that my mom's a lesbian? How would they have treated me, the lesbian's daughter?"

I waited a second, then said, "Maybe to real friends, it wouldn't have made any difference."

"That's bullshit."

"It doesn't make any difference to me."

"Because you can make out with me every night."

I thought about that, letting it sink in, and my blood started to churn. I gave the steering wheel a mighty thump. "Is that what you think? I'm ignoring your mom and Diane so I can make out with you?"

"Let me out at the park," she said.

I understood why Angel wanted her mom and Diane kept a secret, but I didn't believe she could go her entire life lying. I don't care if she became an all-America basketball player and played in the WBA, she'd never be happy.

"Want to know something else?" I said.

"What?"

I didn't hesitate. "I told my dad I was seeing you. It seemed like the right thing to do. You might as well know that, too."

"Fuck!" she said under her breath. "You promised. We made a deal, Danny. How could you?"

"He's my dad, I had to."

She let out the longest sigh. "Once you tell someone a secret it's no longer a secret, did you know that? And it spreads, sometimes accidentally. Like someone overhears someone else whispering. But it spreads, believe me. Sometimes like wildfire. And what people don't know, they make up."

"Hey, I didn't say a word about your mom and Diane,

but"—I sucked in a breath, wondering if I should say this— "he already knew."

She didn't seem surprised. "How?"

I told her about her mother and Dunlap working for the same real estate agency. "Some teachers know, but they haven't talked," I said, "and they won't."

"It won't be long before they all know the truth, will it, Danny?"

"I'll keep my mouth shut."

"You told your dad about us. Who's next? Your football buddies? Your friends Tony and Melody?"

"No one else."

"Right."

She didn't realize I'd bypassed the park, until I stopped in front of her house. Even in the city, the stars were bright.

She cast a glance at her house. Two lights on. One in the living room. I couldn't tell where the other came from. Bedroom, maybe.

"I am so late I don't know how I'm going to explain this," she said. "I told you to let me out at the park."

"I'll come in with you," I said, "and talk to your mom."

"My mom would adore you. She's not the problem."

"You're hiding behind a wall," I said. "And I'm trapped there with you."

Her chin jutted. "You can jump the wall any time you want, Danny. I can't. Good night."

"My dad asked to meet you."

She ignored me. That made me mad.

I didn't help her out of the Jeep. Didn't walk her to the door. Just sat there, numb, and watched to make sure she got into the house okay. I hoped she'd at least tell her mother she'd been with me tonight.

Marshmallows, tiny fire, moonlight—I'd had such high hopes.

I didn't know what to do now.

18.

"Let me guess," Tony said. "Your love life crash-dived."

"Worse than that."

Tony turned off the truck radio. "I've never seen you look so bad, except maybe when you missed those free throws against Burlington, and we lost the first game of the season." He tilted his head. Eyed me. "No, I think you look worse today, buddy."

I had just climbed into his truck in the parking lot at school Monday morning. It was a gray, drizzly day. Tony had had only a second to survey me. Was it that obvious how rotten I felt?

"Wish I could tell you the whole story," I said, "but I can't."

"The Stone Angel?"

"Better if I don't say a word."

"You want my advice, forget her. Cut your losses." He stowed his clipboard, pencil. "But you missed out on Bambi. She's going to the prom with Kevin Brandt. Stinocher didn't have a lock on her after all."

"Never figured falling for a girl could be so complicated."

"Look, she's the first girl you ever went ape over. You're not expected to fall in love with the first one forever. There's others, and some of them like you. I can't imagine why, big stupid nerd like you."

Tony clicked his door open, I reached for mine, and we headed through the drizzle to class.

The Mississippi River would dry up before Angel called me. She wouldn't search me out in school, either. I could cut my losses by not calling her. Tony was right. A guy doesn't fall in love forever with the first girl he goes ape over.

Still, Monday night, I sat in my bedroom at my computer desk with the cordless in my hand, index finger poised to punch Angel's numbers out because . . . because I liked Angel McPherson. Liked her not just to make out with. I think I loved her, though I still hadn't said it to her. She was a cool, fun-to-be-with girl when she wasn't stressed about her mom.

It wasn't as if Angel had been cheating on me with my best friend, Tony. And what kind of guy dumps a girl he thinks he's falling in love with at the first sign of trouble? Angel needed help, that's what. She needed to see that her hiding was self-destructive. But who was I to step in and save her? Could I perform a miracle? I didn't think so. I'd already meddled enough in her life. People save themselves. Nobody does it for them. Maybe she didn't want to be saved.

I laid the phone on the desk. I didn't call.

Tuesday I played golf after school with Dad and Mr. Castle. Mr. Castle and I were ambling off the eighteenth hole together, pulling our carts, Dad a yard behind us, grumbling. The sun had slipped halfway behind the trees.

I'd shot lousy. High eighties, along with Dad, while Mr. Castle had carded a seventy-three.

I think Mr. Castle was trying to change the subject of

golf scores and stop Dad's grumbling, when he said, "Got yourself a date for the prom Saturday night?"

I would have rather talked about golf scores.

"Not me," I said, and wiped the sweat off the back of my neck with a red bandanna. "The one I asked turned me down."

"And who might that be? She must be crazy."

"A blond," is all I said.

He thought a moment. "Angel McPherson, I'll bet, the girl who beat you in the charity assembly. She's not your type, anyway, Danny. She's best left alone."

Another teacher who knew about Angel's mom.

I stuffed my bandanna into my back pocket.

"Lot more women out there," he said, and whacked me hard on the back. "At least you're not like your dad." He chuckled. "I married a woman. They're not half bad."

Driving home from the golf course in Dad's Expedition, he said, "Heard what you said to Castle. A blond turned you down for the prom. Been wondering, you hadn't said anything about it. In fact, you've hardly said a word lately."

"Sunday night was a disaster, and you were asleep when I got home. I haven't felt like talking about it."

"Figured that." He braked for a stoplight. "Look, I don't care for females. I've always made myself clear about that. But just because I'm not interested doesn't mean you can't be. I know part of me's rubbed off on you, but—"

The light changed. The Expedition surged forward.

"I like females—" I halted. "I mean, I like girls, Dad. It hasn't all rubbed off."

"Dunlap will be glad this thing is over."

"What's it got to do with him?"

"Some kids have been talking. Someone saw you two together."

"A cheerleader," I said. "Bambi Powers."

"Dunlap's your coach. Lee keeps pressuring him to keep you away from her star. He comes to me and wants to know if anything's going on between you two."

"None of his business."

"He'll be glad to know you're finished with her, anyway. Keep that female he goes with off his back."

Dad stopped for a girl turning left in front of him in a little red convertible. She'd zipped past us only a minute before, a blond, hair flying. I could picture my mom in a sporty car like that, cruising around town.

I bit my bottom lip and surprised myself, saying, "How did you and mom meet? You've never told me."

This is the kind of stuff he never talked about, clamming up whenever I asked. But now, I thought, I'm not letting us out of this vehicle, Dad, until you tell me.

The girl in front of Dad scooted left, and Dad eased his foot onto the accelerator. His beefy fingers flexed on top of the steering wheel.

"What difference does it make?"

"She was my mom. I'd like to know about her."

We went a block before he said slowly, "All right." Big sigh. "All right." More finger flexing on the steering wheel. "Met her in college in the library. We both wanted to check out the same book. She was from Saginaw, too— you already know that. But she went to Arthur Hill, not Saginaw High, like I did. And she already had a boyfriend at State with her. From Saginaw."

"Max Fowler?"

He nodded. "They'd been going together since high school."

"You stole her away from him?"

"I thought so. She married me after my senior year of football, even though a busted knee ended my thoughts of a pro career."

"Maybe she loved you because you were you, not some big-time football player."

"She had a funny way of showing it."

He fell silent. He made a left turn onto Telegraph Road. We were nearly home, the sun casting long tree-shadows on the road. I knew he wouldn't break the silence, so I said, "What happened?"

"Happened?"

"To you and Mom? Your marriage?"

More silence. He was scowling. I think he was choosing words carefully now, putting them together in his brain in sentences.

"Your mom liked good times," he said. "I was gone a lot. That's the way it is with a teacher starting out. Not much money. I taught PE, coached football and baseball. I refereed high school wrestling meets on weekends. Still not much money."

"She got lonely," I said.

"She knew what was up when she married me. Plenty of teachers work extra hours, and their wives don't take up with their ex-boyfriends. She was bored."

I had him talking. I wasn't going to quit now. "I was an accident?"

He pulled into our driveway. The garage door rumbled up. By the look on his face, I could tell it hurt him to remember.

"A total surprise," he said, leaning back in his seat. "She accused me of messing with her birth control pills. I hadn't, of course, but I thought you were the greatest thing that ever happened."

"And she didn't."

He looked at me.

"Tell me," I said. "I think I've got it figured out, anyway."

He patted my leg. "I honestly think she tried hard for both our sakes. Some things aren't meant to be."

"What was she like?" I said before he could get away. "Did she like sports? Did she bake things?"

I thought his bottom lip quivered. "Her smile was as wide as her face, and she laughed a lot. She didn't cook much. She could sing and dance like crazy. She liked parties."

Then he reached for his door handle, and I knew this conversation had ended. I opened my door and slipped out of the Expedition.

Mom had cheated on him, but I noticed he hadn't called her any names like "slut" or "whore." If she hadn't died, maybe she and Dad could have worked things out between them. And then I remembered what he'd just said. Some things aren't meant to be. I felt sad, but I fought it, thinking, Who needs a mom, anyway? I'm doing okay. But I wished Mom and I would have had a chance.

Saturday morning, I convinced myself I should call Angel, just to see if she had changed her mind a little. Give us another chance. I mean, what if she'd changed her mind about our situation, but was reluctant to call? Was just waiting for me to call? If I didn't step up to help her, who else would? Nobody. She'd go on forever, hiding, hiding, hiding.

I knew for sure Angel wasn't going to the prom tonight. I could probably find her at home. But she might throw me out on my ear. Then I'd know for sure it was over between us.

Some things aren't meant to be.

19.

You sure you want to do this, Danny?

I stood on Angel McPherson's front porch late Saturday afternoon, clutching a long-stemmed red rose wrapped in green tissue. I eyed the doorbell. Licked my lips. I gave the button a jab with my thumb, almost hoping the bell did not ring or chime, feeling my stomach knot up.

It chimed, but no one answered.

The rose seemed like a good idea at the time. Girls freaked over roses. I'd seen them gush with appreciation in movies and TV commercials when a guy handed one of them a flower, and I remembered Tony had used the technique once when Melody was mad at him because he'd ditched her and had gone out with the guys. He said the result of his thoughtfulness was spectacular

So there I stood, punching Angel's doorbell a third time, feeling stupid with a flower in my hand, fighting that knot in my stomach, praying someone would answer so I could hurry this up, when a voice behind me, low and soft, startled me.

"Yes? May I help you?"

Wheeling, trying to put my face together into a smile, I stared at a blond woman dressed in jeans and a long-sleeved denim shirt, sleeves rolled up on freckled arms, muddy gloves on her hands. She was forty, maybe, but beautiful.

I blinked in admiration. "Hi. I'm . . . I'm Danny Henderson." Man, stumbling over my own name—how cool was that?

Her blond hair was piled high on her head. She smiled at me. "Yes, of course. I've been wanting to meet you," she said. "I'm Kathleen McPherson."

Angel's mother.

Her eyes were blue, not gray like Angel's, and her mouth didn't have that little tilt that Angel's had.

"Is Angel home?"

"I thought I heard someone." She waved a hand. "Look at me, such a sight. I've been working on the flowers along the side of the house. Tulips. Gladiola." She stripped off her gloves, shoved them into the back pocket of her jeans, and swiped her forehead with the back of her hand, smearing a smudge of dirt.

"Um . . . is Angel home?" I repeated, and cleared my throat. "I've got this flower—"

"Oh, how lovely."

I felt awkward with that dumb rose in my hand. I stepped aside as Mrs. McPherson glided up the porch steps and took the rose from me. "Come in. We'll put this in water. Angel's not home at the moment."

Mrs. McPherson pulled open the screen door. I hesitated. Bit my bottom lip. Maybe now was the time to split. The rose had been delivered. When she saw it, Angel would know I cared for her as much as ever. She'd call me. No, she wouldn't.

"Please come in," Mrs. McPherson said. "I don't know how to thank you."

Thank me!

I followed her into the house. She was tall and slender, a gentle sway to her hips when she walked, like Angel's sway. She could've been Angel's older sister. Three blue combs held her hair high on her head.

This lady's gay? I can't believe it.

"Sit down," she said. "I'll be right back."

She headed for the kitchen.

The plaid couch, where I'd stretched out Angel over a month ago, sat across the room. I eased into a matching chair just inside the door and, for the first time, took a good look around: a big mirror on one wall, plush carpeting and furniture, a stone fireplace. I hadn't focused on any of that my first time here, but the thing that impressed me now was the vines.

Dainty vines crept out of tiny teapots and colored clay pots that sat on the fireplace mantel and on a coffee table. Other vines hung suspended from wall and ceiling baskets, their long runners and heart-shaped leaves curling everywhere. A giant vine in a huge blue ceramic urn lurked in a corner, its green leaves scaling a bark-covered slab of wood.

I was impressed.

When Mrs. McPherson returned, a glass of iced pop in one hand, the rose in a tall, thin, crystal vase in the other, I was still gawking.

"Aren't vines lovely?" she said, and smiled. Her smile flashed, just like Angel's. She had shed her denim shirt and was now wearing a white T-shirt. She'd wiped the smudge of dirt off her forehead. "So green and climby. I've always loved vines. They help create such a homey atmosphere."

"They're cool."

"Something to drink?" she said. "Pepsi?"

She handed me the glass, its icy wetness cold on my palm. I gulped a drink. She set the vase with the rose in it on the mantel. Her gloves were missing from the back pocket of her jeans.

"Thank you," I mumbled after swallowing. The Pepsi felt good sliding down my dry throat.

"Just a second."

She was back in an instant with a plateful of cookies in her hand.

"Chocolate chip," she said. "Diane bakes all the time. Please have some."

She stood in front of me. I took one.

"Please," she said.

I took one more. She set the plate on a coffee table, and I bit into a cookie. Chocolate chip with nuts. I loved it. No homemade cookies at my house.

"This is great," I said. "Thank you."

I finished off my first cookie and started on the second.

"You'll have to thank Diane," she said, settling on the couch. "And I can't thank you enough for helping Angel when she broke her ankle—getting her home, putting ice on it for her."

"Mrs. McPherson—" I started.

"I can't imagine what would've happened if you hadn't been around."

"Mrs. McPherson, I broke her ankle. I kept her from playing with some all-stars this summer. And I apologize, I feel bad about what happened."

"Nonsense. It was an accident. Angel told me so herself."

I took another drink, two big gulps. Looked at her.

She's not a lesbian. Can't be.

Would my mom have been that beautiful, had she lived?

"I was banging Angel pretty good," I said. I halted. Cleared my throat. "I don't mean banging. I mean, I was shoving her around, trying to prove she had to get physical underneath. You know, in basketball, underneath the basket, when you're rebounding."

Mrs. McPherson slid to the edge of the couch. "You want my opinion, Danny, I think Angel needed a rest from competitive basketball, anyway." She stood. "May I get you another drink?"

I stared into the bottom of my glass. Nothing but melting ice. I hadn't realized I'd drunk all the pop in about three gulps and had devoured my second cookie.

I stood up, too. "No, thank you, Mrs. McPherson. I've got to get going."

She took the glass from me and set it on the coffee table.

"I just wanted to leave that rose with Angel," I said.

Mrs. McPherson tucked stray wisps of hair back up on the pile on her head. "Have you and Angel been seeing each other on a regular basis?"

She sensed my hesitation.

"It's all right," she said. "Don't be afraid. I've encouraged Angel to form friendships at school and to date."

"I'm not exactly afraid."

"It's that Angel doesn't want you to say anything, isn't it?"

I eased back down into my chair, dropped my head back, and stared at the ceiling a moment. Then I looked at Mrs. McPherson again. "Angel's uptight about . . ." I didn't know how to say it.

Mrs. McPherson sat on the very edge of the couch, hands laced on her knees. "Has Angel told you about me? I know you've met Diane."

"A little. Well, quite a lot, actually."

"Her efforts to hide Diane and me have caused major

stress for all of us. But I'm not blaming her, I don't want you to think that. It's my fault for creating a situation where she feels she needs to lie."

"I think if she hadn't lost her dad in that helicopter crash," I said, "if she had him to turn to sometimes, maybe things would be easier for her. I think she misses him a lot. I miss my mom." I suddenly realized I'd have to give an honest explanation. "She died in a motorcycle accident, my mom. Pretty tragic." I shrugged.

"I'm so sorry."

"Helicopter crash, motorcycle accident—Angel and I both have had bad luck with parents."

The saddest look surfaced in Mrs. McPherson's eyes when I mentioned the helicopter crash. It was hard to understand how such a beautiful woman could fall in love with a man, have a kid, then end up in the arms of other women. But her eyes looked so sad and her face sagged so much that I believed she still had feelings for the dead man.

"I hate wearing a mask," she said. "I've always been open about who I am." Deep sigh. "I've lied for Angel's sake, yet for a long while, I've believed I've been doing the wrong thing."

"Eventually Angel's got to tell the truth."

"'Just wait till high school's over,' she keeps begging me. 'I'll be gone.'" Glassy tears pooled in Mrs. McPherson's eyes. "All the lies, that's the one thing I wish I could take back."

"Well, Angel's been pretty honest with me," I said. "Problem is she wants to hide from everyone else, so we have to hide together."

Again that sad look.

I said, "Life hasn't been easy for Angel, has it?"

"Sometimes it's been cruel, and every day I ask myself if I had the right to put her though all this. At least she's opened up to you a little, that's something."

"When will Angel be home? Is she with Diane?"

"Diane volunteers at a homeless shelter. They need help the most on Saturday nights. She goes early."

I nodded.

Mrs. McPherson wrung her hands, looking a little fearful even. "What else has Angel told you about her father?"

"He started a stuffed animal collection for her."

Mrs. McPherson looked right at me, shoulders squared, chin up, as if she were going to tell me something straight out, making no apologies. Then she suddenly turned away, and her shoulders slumped.

"What is it, Mrs. McPherson?"

She blew out a breath. "I have to be honest. I'm not *Mrs.* Please call me Katie, all my friends do." The frown on her face cut deep lines in her forehead and around her lips. It was worse than the frown on Dad's face when we lost a close football game.

"What's wrong?" I said.

Then it hit me that maybe Angel's mom and dad had never been married, Angel was illegitimate, and she was ashamed of that. But that was no big deal. I knew three or four kids at school whose parents weren't married.

Something else was going on here, something big, maybe, but I had no idea what.

"You seem to be a nice young man, Danny. I do hope all this hasn't frightened you. Angel needs a good friend."

"I want to be one," I said, honestly. "And more."

"She thinks she's, well, frankly, she thinks she's a freak, but she's not. She's a lovely, talented girl."

"Why a freak? What else is she hiding?"

Katie's eyes lowered, closed a moment. I watched her throat move as she swallowed. "I can't tell you. I can't destroy her trust in me."

I thought about that. "I know," I said. "I promised Angel I wouldn't tell anyone we were seeing each other, but I betrayed her by telling my dad. I don't think she'll ever forgive me."

"Angel was here when you arrived," Katie said. "She saw your Jeep, came out the back door, and told me to send you away. I couldn't do it. I needed to talk to you, and you need to talk to her."

"That's why I'm here. Why I brought that rose."

"She's been so despondent lately, and for a while, she was beaming around here every day, a ray of sunshine."

"We had a huge disagreement last Sunday and haven't spoken since."

"I thought as much, but she wouldn't tell me. Had you been seeing her during the evenings when she went out?"

I nodded. "For a couple of weeks. Where is she now?" I stood up. "The park?"

Katie pushed herself up from her chair. Smoothed out her jeans. "I doubt it. She has a place along the creek where she goes when she wants to be alone. Right behind our house, across the bike path, to the left, is a little trail. That's probably where you'll find her."

"What else is she hiding?"

Katie shook her head and brushed tears out of her eyes. "Talk to her, Danny."

20.

Angel sat in the grass on the creek bank, plinking stones into the water. Beavers had dammed up the creek, creating a pool in front of her that trickled over the dam. I'll bet the pool was twenty yards across and deep enough to hold fish.

I'd tiptoed along the path, winding through the trees, and had come up behind Angel without her hearing or seeing me.

First thing I noticed was that her crutches were nowhere in sight, not beside her on the bank or anywhere else that I could see. She must have hobbled out of the house in such a panic that she'd left them behind.

I didn't call her name, simply walked up behind her.

She wore purple shorts and a white T-shirt, her hair in pigtails, something different, her legs sprawled out over the bank.

I sat down beside her in the grass, without a word. Her head didn't snap around. I hadn't startled her. Maybe she expected me. She didn't say anything, either. I felt around in the grass, but couldn't find a stone to toss into the water.

A blue walking cast clutched her right ankle and foot. How about that! What a piece of good news.

"Is that you, Angel McPherson?" I said. "The Stone Angel?"

"You're not funny."

"This is me, Danny Henderson."

She blew out a tiny breath.

"What are you doing here?" she said.

"Talking to you."

"Fuck you."

"Another nice day," I said, and leaned back on my hands. "Sunny. Lots of blue sky. Cool breeze here in the shade. Peaceful. Only the sound of birds and the water." I sniffed. "Creek smells a little muddy, though."

"What do you want, Danny?"

"Nice cast. I like the color. Won't be long, you'll be playing basketball again."

"You been practicing your free throws?"

"Frankly, I haven't. I've been distracted."

"If you were committed, nothing would stop you."

"I'm committed to you."

That silenced her. She still hadn't looked at me. She rocked back and forth a little. Two small birds chased a crow across the sky, dive-bombing it.

"What did my mom have to say?"

"She thinks I'm a nice guy. And that you need a friend."

"Isn't that surprising."

"Diane makes the best chocolate chip cookies in the world."

No answer.

"I've missed you, Angel."

"I told you not to call. I didn't think in my wildest dreams you'd come marching up to my front porch."

"You have this bad habit of ignoring me whenever you want. As if I don't exist. Did you see what I brought you?"

"No." Still not looking at me. "Danny, we've had a terrific time. I really, really do like you. I keep telling you that." Her fingers started twining, untwining. "But we can't see each other anymore. I'm not going to explain why again. We gave it a try, we can say that."

"Once you said you loved me."

No answer.

"You want to be left alone, right? And you want me to keep my mouth shut."

Angel thought if people knew all about her, she'd be rejected outright. She'd be isolated and lonely. So she'd built a wall around herself, and she defended that wall, but she was still isolated and lonely.

What kind of sense did that make?

I gave a dry little laugh. "You don't want to be hurt by what people will say, but you're hurting yourself."

"Why don't you stay out of my life, Danny?"

"I've liked you since the moment I saw you last October, getting a drink of water at the fountain near the office. I asked Tony who you were. 'New stud on the girls' basketball team,' he said."

"You should've minded your own business."

I kicked at the side of the bank with my heel. A soft clump of dirt tumbled into the creek. "Remember, I told you I lied to you about my mom, then I told you the truth, remember? Here's more of the truth. In school, I used to pretend my women teachers were my mom. I liked the pretty teachers best. I had two really pretty ones, one in first grade, another in fourth.

"And listen to this. In fourth grade, our class was taking a field trip to the museum, and when I was getting off the bus, I tripped and fell out the door right onto the concrete sidewalk. I was okay, didn't scrape anything, not even my nose or knees, wasn't even crying, but Miss Kramer grabbed me and hugged me and pressed my head right into her chest, soft and cottony. 'Are you all right, Danny?' she cooed. 'Are you all right?' Was I all right? Was she kidding? I'll never forget that, my head buried in her boobs."

"Why are you telling me this?"

"I even wrote letters to my dead mother and read them over her grave. That's the truth, too."

"I don't want to know anything else about you."

Time for more full-court pressure.

"Look, Angel, everyone buries secrets. But sometimes we reveal them to people we like . . . love. Can trust."

"I can't trust you. I can't even trust my mom."

"Let all the secrets go, Angel."

"What did my mom tell you?"

"Is there something else to tell? Something more than your mother's being a lesbian?"

"What did she say?"

"You tell me."

"She told you, didn't she?"

"Told me what? Say it yourself!"

Angel collapsed backward into the grass, her right forearm flung across her eyes. "This is terrible," she mumbled.

"She said you think of yourself as being a freak. She said—"

"All right! Fuck it!" Angel exploded. "I'm a test-tube baby!" She said it to the sky, her arm still flung over her eyes. "Now you know! Got it? Satisfied? Get out. Scream it across the state."

"What?" I must have blinked a million times in the next three seconds, trying to compute what she'd just said. "What?"

"My mom was artificially inseminated," Angel said. "I'm a sperm donor's kid. A guy who I've never met, not by letter, phone, or e-mail. Will never meet. Ever."

That one was a shocker. I fell back into the grass alongside Angel, her arm still covering her eyes.

"You came from a test tube?" I said.

"Makes me a fucking freak, doesn't it?"

"You are *not*—I repeat—*not* a freak."

"You want me to draw you a picture? I'm the result of a donor's semen, which was placed in a test tube and held at a sperm bank until someone made a request and met certain qualifications."

"Your mom?"

"Now you're getting smarter, Danny. Hard to believe?"

It was, but I said, "No. I just hadn't thought about it before."

"Know anyone else conceived like I was?"

"No," I admitted.

"Makes me a freak. Right?" Her voice was tight with held-back tears.

And then it began to sink in, what it all meant. Angel was double different. Her mom was a lesbian, and Angel herself was a test-tube baby. She had no dad in the Army who died in a helicopter crash. No dad at all. Not in a normal sense. No wonder she wanted to at least appear normal. Nearly everything about her was a lie. Except basketball.

"Is that why," I said, "you've become such a dedicated basketball player, to prove your worth?"

"I absolutely hate you for making this so difficult. Leave me alone!"

I rolled onto my side, smelling the grass and earth, elbow on the ground, my head propped in my hand. She was silent, perfectly still, but I could tell she was crying. I could see tears leaking from underneath her forearm and tracking down her cheeks. I hated seeing her cry.

I inched up close, smelling the light lilac scent of her hair. A little breeze blew. I wanted to stroke her cheek, but didn't.

"The prom's out for tonight," I said. "That's obvious. How about a movie? Then Sunday afternoon, we go to the park and work on my free throws. Monday morning I come by and pick you up for school, and we walk into school holding hands."

I stopped. Waited for her response.

She lay motionless in the grass, arm still clamped over her eyes.

I picked a blade of grass and tickled her lips with it. That got her attention. She flinched, went *pffft!* with her mouth, and swiped at my hand.

She sat up, finally, and stared at me. "Haven't you been listening to me?"

"The part about your being a test-tube baby? Sure. It doesn't make you a freak, though. Just a beautiful girl I'm crazy about. Let's show everyone what a hot couple we are."

"That's the same stupid plan you had before."

"It'll work. Nothing else has. Not lying or hiding. I'll buy a gross of condoms."

That earned me an icy stare, and I gave her a stony look back. "Was the stuffed animal collection a lie, too?"

She maneuvered herself to her knees and stood up, putting weight on her right foot. It must have been feeling a lot better. Good.

I jumped up. "No stuffed animal collection, right?"

"Right." Tiny sigh.

She brushed grass off her bottom, legs, arms. Touched her lips, probably thinking that blade of grass I'd tickled her with was stuck there.

"My mom tell you she named me Angel because she thought I was truly a gift from God?"

"Cool," I said. "Now that you've told me all the truth, you'll get your halo back."

"I wish I'd never met you. You're the worst big mistake of my life."

She turned and started clumping along, through ankle-high grass, to the trail.

I called her name. She didn't respond.

She was ignoring me again. That's how she dealt with me when she couldn't handle me. She ignored me, as if I didn't exist, as if I'd go away.

I was getting tired of that. I felt my face getting red like Dad's does at football practice when he's mad at some guy for missing an assignment, and he gets in the guy's face. Sometimes he'll grab the guy's face mask and nearly twist his head off. He's done that to me.

Angel was twenty yards away when I fired a shot at her. "You *are* worthless, aren't you? You're a worthless fraud! The world's biggest liar."

That halted her. She whirled and faced me, fists jammed into her hips. Then she stalked toward me, wounded, face on fire, gray eyes dark and angry.

She skidded to a stop in front of me and slapped me hard with her open hand. I was so surprised, so caught off balance, that I stumbled two steps backward and toppled off the bank into four feet of muddy water in the beavers' pool. I sank all the way to the bottom on my back and swallowed ten gallons of creek water before I came up spitting and sputtering. So mad I could hardly see.

Angel was gone. Flown away for good this time, by God, I hoped, as I climbed up the creek's muddy bank onto the grass.

Gone for good.

I'd done my best and failed.

Man, was I wet and muddy. And smelled of fish and creek water.

My cheek burned as if Angel had left her palm print there forever.

She was a snapping turtle.

And I'd learned my lesson. Finally.

After I'd dragged myself out of the beaver pond, I sprinted along the trail and across Angel's yard to my Jeep, and made my getaway before Katie could rush out of the house to stop me. Made a muddy mess of the Jeep's front seat. Had no sheet or anything to use as a cover.

When I got home, I couldn't avoid Dad. He was in the garage, restringing fishing reels. He dropped the one in his hand on the workbench. "What happened to you?" he said, and laughed. "You look like a drowned rat."

"Fell into the creek."

No use denying it. I looked like I'd fallen into the creek. Soaking wet. Mud everywhere. Hair, shirt, shorts, shoes. I wondered if Angel's palm print was still seared on my cheek.

"You haven't done that since you were a kid."

"I had some help this time."

"Angel McPherson?"

"You won't have to worry about her any longer. I hate her."

As soon as I said that, I knew it wasn't true. I didn't hate her. I just—I don't know how I felt about her. As if I needed to stay away from her, I guessed. And sick about the way things had turned out.

21.

Bambi's best friend, Kristin Logan, threw a party at her house the Friday after the Big Slap. "What's the occasion?" I asked, when Bambi called me at home about four o'clock, the day of the party, and asked if I'd go with her.

At first her voice sounded so much like Angel's my heart skipped, then rattled around in my chest. I'd vowed again to forget Angel, and my heart's getting excited like that ticked me off. I didn't want Angel to have that effect on me any longer.

Bambi said, "No special occasion—sorry about such short notice. You have plans already?"

"None that I can think of."

"Kristin's parents are out of town for the weekend. What do you think?"

"Are you a snapper?"

"What? What's a snapper?"

"Nothing," I said. "Just a little goofy today."

"Like, do I bite?"

"Look, I don't even know why I said that."

"I bite a little bit," she said. "But not very hard. You're not scared, are you? How about to night?"

I debated precisely a second. "I wouldn't miss Kristin's party."

"Cool."

I knew Tony and Melody wouldn't be at the party because they had tickets for a Parasites concert at the Mark, a group Melody insisted was a must-see. But I called Tony right away to tell him Bambi and I were finally going out.

"You're moving up in the world," he said. "Melody will freak when I tell her. Hope you can handle Bambi. She's hot."

"Don't worry, I'll take care of her."

"Think of all the time you wasted with the Stone Angel."

"She's a fraud. Totally. Someday I might be able to tell you the whole story."

"I'm dying to hear it. Good luck tonight, buddy. But you probably won't need it."

"Thanks."

"Not a guy with all your experience."

We both laughed at that, and hung up.

I picked up Bambi at her house that night, seven-thirty. It had been a sweltering day, the first hot, hot one of the year, but I could tell the evening would be cool and pleasant. Getting close to Bambi would be a perfect way to forget Angel.

Bambi didn't wait for me to come up to her front door and get her. She came flying out of the house the moment I stopped, and popped into the Jeep, wearing white shorts and a white polo shirt, smelling like a whole bouquet of flowers. Gardenias, maybe.

"Just a second," she said, a little breathless.

She pulled the visor down, peered at herself in the mirror, moistened her lips with her tongue. She searched in her purse for a tiny gold tube, then carefully smeared plum-dark lipstick on her lips. Finished, she fluffed her curly red hair, then flipped up the visor.

"Ready," she said, and smiled at me. Tiny pearl earrings nestled in her earlobes.

I'd never seen Angel with makeup on or jewelry. A true angel doesn't need all that.

"Were you surprised to hear from me?" Bambi said.

I started the jeep and eased it into gear. "Well, let me see. At the Wapsi, I saw you with Pete Stinocher, and the last thing I heard is you went to the prom with Kevin Brandt."

"Yeah, well, I'm trying to be more selective these days. I'm tired of going out with world-class jerks."

"How do you know I'm not one? A world-class jerk?"

"I don't, I just know I don't want anymore of those two."

Kristin's party was downstairs in the rec room. I'd seen Kristin around school because she was a cheerleader and student senate president.

Bambi and I went in through the raised garage door, then down the stairs where the party was already wound up. Laughter and loud music made it almost impossible to hear. Smoke hung so thick in the air it made my eyes sting. I was sure I smelled weed. Flashes of blue, green, yellow, and white lights slashed across the walls and ceiling of the otherwise dim rec room.

As soon as Kristin spotted Bambi and me, I got a feeling I might be out of place here. Kristin sang out at the top of her lungs, "Look who's here, guys! Bambi and the Incredible Hulk! Get 'em a beer, somebody!"

In this flashing darkness, I hoped no one could see me blushing.

"Here are the ground rules," Kristin shouted at us. "Party's inside, not outside. Down here, not upstairs. I don't want the neighbors to hear. They'll call the cops. I can't trash the whole house because I'll never get it cleaned up before my parents get back."

A guy in cut-off jeans, white T-shirt, and suspenders

pressed a cold can of Old Milwaukee into my hand and one into Bambi's.

"Thanks," I said.

"You ever done it on a waterbed?" Kristin asked me.

"What?" I bent closer to her.

She smirked at me and slapped Bambi on the shoulder. "Where do you get these guys?"

"This one's different."

"Right. My new waterbed's upstairs. You can use it. A deal I would offer only to my best friends." She pecked a kiss off Bambi's cheek.

Bambi said, "Thanks," and studied her can of Old Mil.

I popped my can open, cleared my throat, and chugged half of it down. Might as well have a really good time while I was at it. The beer was so cold my teeth tingled.

I heard a glass smash, a girl scream, and then a male voice shouting above the noise, "Hey, Kristin! You got a mop?"

"Shit!" Kristin said, and disappeared.

Someone put slow-dance music in the CD player, and Bambi said, "Want to?"

"Sure."

I finished off my Old Mil with a second chug, and set the empty can on the bar. Bambi placed hers on the bar, too. Unopened.

She reached up, circled her arms around my neck—a long stretch for her—and snuggled her body close to mine. When she tucked her head of curly hair under my chin, her gardenia scent overpowered the room's smoky smell.

Along with three or four other couples, lights splashing across us, we danced close, swaying, feet shuffling over the carpeted floor—I wasn't bad at this kind of dancing. I closed my eyes and tried to picture Bambi and me later tonight on Kristin's waterbed—my first time—but Angel's image kept replacing Bambi's. Angel with her blond hair and tilted mouth.

I blinked and shook my head.

Bambi looked up and said, "Something wrong, Danny?"

"My eyes burn from the smoke."

"We could go outside somewhere. Or upstairs to Kristin's room. But we just got here."

At that moment, the music stopped. Bambi raised herself up on her tiptoes and kissed me. I leaned into her and kissed her back, wishing I was kissing Angel in front of all these people. I made an extra effort to make that kiss work, practically squeezing Bambi to death, I thought. But her body clinging to mine didn't feel like Angel. Her lips pressing on mine didn't taste like Angel. Her scent flooding my nostrils didn't smell like Angel.

I might have kissed her forever trying to turn her into Angel, but Kristin broke us up.

"Knock it off, you two," Kristin said, and grabbed Bambi's arm.

"What's wrong with you?" Bambi could hardly breathe.

I was a little breathless myself. I wiped my lips with the back of my hand.

"It's Courtney," Kristin said. "She needs help." Then to me, "Sorry, I've got to steal your girl."

Kristin pulled Bambi away into the crowd, and suddenly I was left alone. The party was getting louder, more crowded, and I wondered why I wasn't feeling happier. I asked a thin-faced guy with glasses where the beer was. He pointed to the open door of the utility room with a washer, dryer, and water heater inside. In a corner, under a blanket, sat a tub of iced Old Mil, cheapest supermarket beer in the world.

I grabbed one and chugged it.

I grabbed another and decided to wander.

Five guys and two girls were seated around two card tables pushed together, playing Quarters. The game is simple, unless you're drunk. You set a short glass with a wide rim in front of you and try to bounce a quarter off the table into the glass, one try only. If you miss, you have to take a slug of beer. If you make it, you designate someone else to take a slug, usually the guy who gets bombed the easiest. Then you pass the glass and quarter to the next player. The more players, the more fun.

I watched for a while, they asked me to play, but I said I didn't think so. I finished my can of Old Mil and grabbed another.

It started to feel hot in the basement. I moved around again. Drums pounded, guitars screamed. Bodies sprawled in chairs or leaned against walls. Couples danced. I finally spotted Bambi and Kristin sitting on a sofa with a tall girl between them. The girl didn't seem able to sit by herself, and her head kept bobbing. I wondered if Bambi and Kristin needed help carrying her someplace. I shuffled off for another beer before offering my services, and bumped headlong into Pete Stinocher, his left cheek bulging with chew.

His face wore a crooked smile. He was drunk.

"So how's Bambi?" He whacked me on the shoulder and scowled, his beer-soaked words a little slurred. "Seen you walk in with her." His paw gripped an Old Mil can, the top cut out so he could spit into it.

"She's fine."

"Fine?"

I wondered if we were going to have a fight over her. *The fewer females . . .*

"You beat me out at tight end," he said, "because your old man's the coach, but you won't do any better with Bambi Powers than I did. She's not worth the effort, man. She's a tease." He spit into his can. "A tease, that's all. Take it from me. And screw you and your old man."

He spit into his can again and drifted off. I popped my Old Mil and took a swig.

I was starting to feel a little loose. Drunk, maybe. I find a wall to lean on. Can't see Kristin or Bambi or the girl with the bobbing head anywhere. Party's really revving up. Everyone's swilling a can of Old Mil. I blink at faces that are smirking, grinning, laughing. Music, beer, flashing lights, smoke—everything's fogging my mind. A tall girl with long blond hair bursts out of the pack of dancers and grabs my hand.

I straighten, my heart pounding so hard I feel it in my throat.

What's Angel doing here?

The girl with the long blond hair pulls me onto the dance floor.

"I didn't see you come in," I say. "I'm so damned happy you're here."

I grab her waist, pull her close, and try to kiss her. She pounds my shoulders with doubled fists, driving me away.

"Hey, dude, back off! I want to dance, that's all."

I stare at her, my eyes out of focus in all this smoke.

"Sorry," I mumble. "It's so dark. Can hardly see..."

I stumble as I climb the basement stairs, leaving the

shrill laughter and pounding music behind me. The smoke, too.

Outside, I stand in the driveway, close my eyes, and throw my head back. I sway and breathe in the fresh air, trying to clear my lungs, ears, and brain. Bright stars flirt with a sliver of moon. I flounder around the flowerbed next to the house and finally plop on the front stoop, head hanging, eyes closed, elbows propped on my knees.

"Are you all right?" I realized Bambi was sitting next to me, an arm around my shoulder. "I saw you go up the stairs. I couldn't get here right away." She touched my cheek with her hand. "You feel flushed."

"Hot down there. Too many beers too fast, I had to come up for air."

"That used to happen to me. That's why I don't drink it anymore. Sorry about leaving you."

"How's Courtney?"

"We persuaded her to go to bed in Kristin's room. She and her boyfriend were fighting. She got into some vodka."

"So much for using Kristin's waterbed."

Bambi nudged my chin with her fingertips, making me face her. "Did you want to?"

"I don't know. Did you?"

Bambi answered me with a kiss. I wrapped her in my arms for the second time that night, drew her close, and kissed her, hard, trying to make myself feel something for her, but my heart was quiet, and my lips soon lost interest. We broke the kiss, releasing each other, and sat apart.

"Sorry," I said. "It's not you."

She started tapping her toe on the concrete, her chin

to him."

"Yeah. He said that. But that has nothing to do—"

"I can't stand that Levi Garret, he crams in his mouth, for one thing, and Kevin Brandt's a pothead. I'm looking for the perfect guy. Melody said it might be you."

"Not hardly."

She paused and looked at me in the dark. "You're still hung up on Angel McPherson, aren't you?"

I shrugged.

"Doesn't it matter to you that her mom's gay? Angel lives with fags."

My mouth dropped. I stared at Bambi. "What? How?"

"Don't tell me you don't know, Danny. Doesn't it make any difference?"

"Who told you that?"

"Why? It's true."

"Who?"

"Your dad, your very own dad."

I started to jump up, but didn't make it. A wave of nausea slapped me down, and I slumped on the stoop again, my head spinning.

"You all right?" Bambi said. "You don't look so good."

I swallowed and held my breath a second. "Tried to get up too quick." I swallowed again. Waited. I didn't want to toss my cookies. Eventually, I said, "My dad would never ever tell you something like that about another student."

"Well, listen to this, Danny. Today our gym class was outside on the diamonds playing softball, last period of the day. Mr. Dunlap's my teacher. My team was in the field. I wasn't playing. Cramps. I was sitting in the dugout. And your dad came over to the fence by third base and started talking to Mr. Dunlap."

dugout. And your dad came over to the fence by third base and started talking to Mr. Dunlap."

I shook my head. "He would not tell you that."

"Listen to me! I got up to ask if I could go back into the building. Use the rest room. I stood behind them. They didn't realize I was there. Your dad's got this big voice, anyway. Are you ready for this?"

I closed my eyes a moment. "Go ahead."

"I heard your dad say he thought it was over between you and the Stone Angel. Then he goes, 'Good thing, since it can't be a healthy lifestyle for her, living in a homosexual environment all her life, and it wouldn't be good for Danny, dating her, being exposed to lesbians.'" Bambi squealed now. "Lesbians! I heard him say that. I nearly died."

"I'll bet."

"That answered my questions about Angel McPherson, why she's so freaky. She has to be gay. She must be, if her mom is."

"Wrong conclusion."

"Anyway, it was obvious you weren't seeing her, so that's why I called right away and asked you to Kristin's party."

I grabbed Bambi's shoulders. "Have you told this to anyone else?"

"A couple of kids. Why? She wants to keep it a big secret, doesn't she? Too bad." Bambi shook her shoulders. "Let go of me."

"It's nobody else's business."

"Let go."

My hands dropped.

"Look, Danny, I'm sorry. I have nothing against her, nothing against you. But your being hung up on her is so weird. So wrong for you."

I rolled Bambi's revelation over and over in my mind. I wished my brain were clearer. Finally, I said, "I'm going home. I don't want to ruin your evening, but I have to go."

Bambi shrugged. "I'm going to stay the night with Kristin, anyway, and help clean up tomorrow. You could stay with me."

I shook my head and felt a buzzing inside.

"Sure you can drive?" she asked. "Maybe you should stay."

"I'll be all right."

She kissed me on the cheek. "If I were you, I'd forget about Angel McPherson. It's so weird, her situation."

And with that, Bambi scooted away, back to the party.

I don't know how long I sat in my Jeep in the dark in front of Kristin's house, trying to sober up, trying to set things straight in my head.

I thumped a fist off the steering wheel. This was terrible. The word was out about Angel's mom and her lover, the worst possible turn of events for Angel. On Monday, gossip would sweep through the school. She'd think I'd told!

If I hadn't forced myself into Angel's life, pressured her to date, none of this would have happened. I was helping ruin her life.

I started the Jeep. Flexed my fingers across the top of the steering wheel.

I had to do something.

What?

22.

It didn't take brains to realize I couldn't put out this fire I'd started. By the time I got home from Kristin's party, I knew the only thing I could do was warn Angel. I'd be there for her if she'd let me. She wouldn't. She'd build a bigger wall. I didn't think she could make it tall enough, though. Or fireproof.

When I crept into the house, Dad was asleep. I drank a gallon of cold water from the fridge. I crawled into bed and tried to formulate a new game plan, realizing the things never worked, but I had to have something in mind.

I didn't call Angel Saturday or Sunday. She'd probably hang up on me, and this was something that had to be hashed out face-to-face. I didn't tromp up to her front door, either, a stupid rose in my hand, like I had last Saturday. That scene had been a disaster.

Sunday afternoon, I wrote her a note on the back of one of those progress charts she'd photocopied for me. First, I marked all the categories on the chart "excellent." That would get her attention.

Then I turned the sheet over and said:

Dear Angel,
     I need to talk to you. Something terrible has happened. Something worse than anything you could ever imagine, and it's been all my fault. Please call me tonight after school so we can meet in the park and talk. This is really a serious situation. I'm sorry about last Sunday. I love you not in spite of who you are

but because of who you are. Does that make sense? I hope so because that's how I feel.

Love,
Danny

Not beautiful but that was the best I could do. Though I always get A's in English, it took me nearly an hour to get those few lines out. I debated a long while over that last part. I didn't know if it sounded stupid or not, but now was not the time to hold back.

Monday morning before school, I opened the door of Tony's truck, stuck my head in, and said, "Got no time. Sorry. Running late."

"Hey, buddy," he said, "haul your ass in here. Guess what I heard." He waved me in.

"Can't. Tell me later."

"What happened at the party Saturday night, you and Bambi—"

I slammed the door. I know what he'd heard. Easy to figure out how it happened. Bambi was a cheerleader. Melody was a cheerleader. They were friends. Mouthy. The fire had started already.

Dodging kids all the way, I raced into school, bounded up the stairwell and down the hall to Angel's locker. My goal was to hand Angel my note personally, slap it right into her palm, so I at least knew she'd received it, certified mail. I waited and waited at Angel's locker, kids passing by, staring at me, until I had only about five minutes left, and knew I had to rush to my own locker for my gear. Damn! Why couldn't something go right just once?

I did the next best thing I could think of. I slipped the note through the air vents at the top of Angel's locker door and hoped she'd find it. Read it.

154

I was so bummed about not finding her, and trying so hard to remember what I needed to take to my classes that morning, only a few minutes left, that I didn't see Angel standing in front of my locker—until I looked up and practically bumped into her.

"Where have you been?" she said.

"What are you doing here?" I couldn't believe she was standing there. I nearly jumped out of my skin.

"Talking to you," she said, and smiled.

"Listen," I said, "I've got to tell you something. It's very important."

"I'll meet you by your Jeep after school. Where is it?"

"Waverly Road. Angel—"

"Got to fly, Danny."

Off she strode on her walking cast into a clot of students.

This was the last week of school. Most classes were doing review work for the first two days, a separate test schedule for the final three days. All morning, questions streaked through my mind at a million miles an hour. I couldn't concentrate on schoolwork. Angel standing there at my locker waiting for me—why?

She wanted to meet me at my Jeep.

What did it all mean?

Had she changed her mind about our relationship?

Was she going to tell the truth? Ignore what people said or thought?

That couldn't be right. Something was wrong here. What, though? What, what, what? Knowing something bad had to happen, but having no idea what it might be, gave me the creepiest feeling.

After second period, I stopped at my locker for a note-book I'd forgotten, and I heard a voice behind me say, "Is that the guy?" I turned immediately and saw another guy point at me and say, "Yeah, that's him. He goes with a queer."

Then they giggled and galloped off. Stupid freshmen. I wanted to run them down and crack their skulls to-gether, but now was not the time to get thrown out of school for fighting.

Just a minute later, on my way to chemistry, I spotted Kristin in the hall by a drinking fountain. I wanted to tell her I was sorry I had to leave her party early, but she looked at me blankly, as if she didn't know me, and scur-ried away before I could get a word out. This was the silent treatment from the girl who was going to let me use her new waterbed.

At lunch, Tony slipped into a seat across from me.

I frowned. "What are you doing here?"

I looked at my pizza. We'd had pizza twice last week. They must have been clearing out the freezer these last few days of school.

"Got to talk to you, buddy."

"You'll get detention, being late for class."

"Can't help it."

"I know what you're going to say about Angel's mom. Bambi told Melody, and she told you, right?"

"You've known a long time, haven't you?"

"Couple of weeks."

"And you didn't tell anyone."

"Uh-uh."

He looked hurt.

"Know what they're saying now?" he asked.

"What?"

He licked his lips. Leaned closer across the table. "There's big lesbian orgies at Angel McPherson's house every night," he said. "You're in on it. They let you watch."

I shoved my pizza to the center of the table. I felt as if I'd been tackled with the football wrapped in my arms, buried in my gut. On a play like that, when you hit the ground, the ball pounds the air out of your lungs. Leaves you twisting on your back, gasping for air.

I caught my breath. "Who said that?"

"It's a rumor. I don't know who started it."

"Bambi? Melody? One of those other cheerleaders?"

"Melody heard it."

"It's not true." I belted a fist off the table. Just like my dad. "Tell everyone you know it's not true. Shout it at the top of your lungs: Not true!"

Tony looked around. "Hey, quiet, buddy. You're getting all excited."

"I'm not supposed to? People saying things and not knowing what the hell they're talking about?"

"No orgies?"

"Tony! Get real!"

"One more thing," he said. He looked sheepish, as if he didn't want to say this. "Is the Stone Angel gay?"

I eyed him. He was my best friend. I felt so sick to my stomach I wanted to puke. "Melody sent you to ask me, didn't she? That's why you're here. She wants to confirm the juicy gossip. Are you that whipped?"

"Don't get sore."

"I can't believe this is happening."

"We're friends, aren't we? We can talk about stuff like this."

"She's not gay," I said. "Hope that doesn't disappoint Melody. Or you."

He sighed. "Look, I should tell you Melody's pissed because she tried to fix you up with a hot girl like Bambi Powers, and you chose a girl who's—"

"What! Who's what?"

His eyes lowered. "Nothing. Melody's feelings are hurt, that's all."

"Too bad."

We sat there in silence a moment. I wanted to pick up the piece of pizza and sling it across the cafeteria. Tony scraped his chair back to leave, and I grabbed his wrist.

"What's this do between you and me?" I said. "Anything?"

"Nothing," he said, and looked right at me. "I don't care who you go out with. The Stone Angel seems cool to me. Whatever."

"You're sure?"

"Man, we're buddies. We're next year's basketball team. We've got to stick together. The Fox and the Bruiser."

"Melody's not going to like that."

He gave a little nod. "She'll learn to live with it."

We shook, and he bailed.

By the time I got to my afternoon classes, I was paranoid. Each person I smiled or nodded at, each person I spoke to—what was that person thinking? Did he or she know? I shook my head. Why was I letting this bother me?

In Mrs. Krohn's seventh-period American lit class, I sat in the front seat, middle row. All during our review of American authors and their contribution to literature, I thought I felt everyone's stare bouncing off my neck and shoulders, a prickly sensation. I couldn't wait to get out of there.

I would have been the first to hit the door when Mrs. Krohn dismissed us, except I knocked my pencil onto the floor, and it rolled away across the front of the room. I got up to retrieve it—should've left it—as everyone rushed by, except Pete Stinocher. When I got up, pencil in my hand, he said softly, in my face, "Fag lover!" His breath smelled like pepperoni.

I didn't even think. It was like I blew a fuse or something. I dropped the pencil. I grabbed him by the T-shirt, bunched it up under his chin, muscled him back, and bopped his head off the blackboard in the front of the room. "Say it again," I growled, "and I'll break your skull."

My face felt on fire.

Mrs. Krohn screamed, "Daniel! Stop that!" and tried to jump in between us, all five-two of her, maybe a hundred forty pounds. Stinocher and I, together, weighed over four hundred pounds.

I released him immediately. I liked Mrs. Krohn. Didn't want to cause her any trouble. Besides, Stinocher held his hands up, palms out, signaling he was innocent of any wrongdoing, didn't know what was happening. He wasn't going to fight. He wouldn't have said anything like that if we had been outside, say in the parking lot, where we could've settled this.

I backed away, breathing hard, and said, "I'm sorry, Mrs. Krohn."

Her face was white. She pointed at Stinocher. "I want you to leave the building at once. Out!"

He gave her a smirk and said with exaggerated politeness, "Yes, Mrs. Krohn."

He turned to leave, and I saw a few faces lingering in the doorway, eyes wide, watching the action, loving it.

Mrs. Krohn pointed at me. "I want you to sit down."

I obeyed and sat in my regular seat.

She strode to the door, slammed it on the lingering faces, then turned to me, arms crossed.

"You want to tell me what that was all about?"

I took in a deep breath and let it out all at once. "He said something I didn't like."

She looked at me hard, tapped her toe on the linoleum floor. She wasn't going to let it go.

I gazed at my desktop, then at her. "He said I was a fag lover."

She blinked. Frowned. Tilted her head. "What in the world is going on?"

"It's nothing, Mrs. Krohn. It was just a joke, and I took it wrong."

"A fag lover?"

She pursed her lips. Was she puzzled? Surely she wasn't going to ask me to explain the phrase "fag lover" like she was always asking everyone to explain similes and metaphors.

"He didn't mean anything by it," I said. "I overreacted. Honest. I'm sorry."

"Danny, I don't know what's going on between you two, but name-calling, fighting—I won't tolerate it in this classroom."

"I understand. It won't happen again." I shifted in my desk. "May I go? Please. Someone's waiting for me."

"You're a nice young man, Danny." She picked up my pencil and handed it to me.

"Thanks."

That curious look again, an eyebrow arched. "I'm sure your dad's very proud of you. Please don't do anything to change that."

I pushed myself out of my desk.

"I won't."

"I mean it, Danny. I don't want you leaving this building looking for a fight."

"I won't."

"Promise?"

"Yes."

"Get out of here."

I rushed out the door and headed down the hallway. What a terrible day. Kids talking behind my back, Kristin blowing me off, Tony eager to hear gossip, Stinocher calling me a fag lover—I couldn't believe it.

23.

Fifty yards down the road from where I stood, Angel perched on the hood of my Jeep, legs crossed, her right foot with the cast on it resting on the bumper.

Every kid leaving school driving down Waverly Road must have seen Angel. Sitting there in the shade from the tall locust trees alongside the road, she couldn't have been more visible.

I expected her to be hidden away inside the Jeep. But there she sat, in yellow shorts and a white blouse, the ultimate hood ornament. A picture of her as Miss June would've been worthy of any car calendar. The Chrysler Motor Corporation would've paid her a million on the spot to advertise on TV.

I sauntered down the hill, feeling a grin on my face, but my happiness suddenly collided with a sense of confusion. Standing in front of my locker this morning, sitting on the hood of my Jeep this afternoon—this wasn't the reclusive Angel I knew.

The sun was hot on my shoulders, and I could smell

the tar from the blacktop. White flowers bloomed in the shallow ditch alongside the shoulder. A good spring for flowers.

"Hi," I said, and halted in front of my Jeep. "You have any idea what you're doing?"

She'd braided her hair into a single long strand, now hanging between her breasts, a ribbon of gold.

"Hi." She dug in the back pocket of her shorts and pulled out a folded piece of paper. She unfolded it and held it out for my inspection. "I want to know what kind of bullshit this is. I found it in my locker at noontime."

I was staring at the progress chart I'd filled out, checking every category "excellent."

"You read the other side?"

Head slightly lowered, eyes raised, she said, "I did."

"I don't know what you think you're doing here, but you're in a heap of trouble. So am I. My fault."

A white Ford Thunderbird with a bunch of kids in it, windows wide open, raced down the hill, raising dust. I swear every kid was staring at Angel and me. At the last minute, one of them waved. I don't know who it was, but I waved back. Angel did, too.

Then she turned to me and said, "You know what happened to me today, what I did?"

"I've got to tell you something first. Maybe you've heard—"

"Uh-uh," she said, interrupting. "Me first."

I put my foot on the Jeep's bumper, leaned against the fender. "Go ahead." I wasn't that eager to tell my story.

She folded the paper, stuck it in her back pocket.

"You were right the other day when you said I was a worthless fraud. The world's biggest liar. Not very nice things to say, though." She gave me a soft smile.

"Sorry about that, I was pretty ticked."

"And I'm sorry about slapping you and you fell into the creek. I think I swung at you and turned around to run all in one motion. I'm not sure I saw you fall in. I don't remember it."

My turn to smile. "I didn't drown. I can swim."

"I saw you climbing into your Jeep. I was peeking out a window in the front of the house, and it dawned on me, you'd fallen in. Mom wanted me to run out and get you, but I wouldn't, I was still so mad."

"I was mad, too. I wouldn't have come in."

Another car zipped by, just a driver, and he honked at us—I don't know who. We both waved.

"What happened to you today?" I said. "My day hasn't been too good."

Angel uncrossed her legs, settling both feet on the bumper, her hands on the hood. "We were reviewing in social studies class, the sixties, discrimination, the civil rights movement, and Miss Goodwin asked if we knew of anyone who had been discriminated against in the workplace. Or if we had, if we had jobs.

"I don't know. I just slammed my pencil down on my desk and thought 'this is it, I'm going to do this.' I raised my hand and said my mom had been discriminated against in the workplace. She's a realtor, and some people won't let her show a house to them when they find out she's a lesbian and has a lover who lives with us."

I caught my breath. "Oh, my God. You didn't! Did you really?"

She nodded her head. "Yes." Kept nodding.

Two motorcycles came screaming up the hill, spokes flashing, clicking, helmetless heads bent low over the bars, hair flying. I don't think they noticed us.

"You did that?" I said. This was awesome. This was frightening.

"I did. I said it wasn't fair because my mother was as good a realtor as anyone else. Maybe better. She's passed the state exam wherever she goes, first try, and makes lots of money, so her lover doesn't have to work."

"Oh, man!"

"Half the class turned around to look at me—I sit in the middle, near the back—mouths hanging open, not believing what I'd said, I guess. Miss Goodwin said that was an excellent example, then went on right away to someone else. When class was over, everyone stood up and sort of parted, like the Red Sea, letting me go first, and I felt everyone's eyes hitting off my back, heard a bunch of whispering."

"I can't believe you did that."

"Isn't that what you wanted me to do?"

"But gradually, you know. Ease into it."

"Right, just ease into saying something like that. Tell me how." She shifted on the hood. Rubbed the dusty red paint with her hand. "Look, when you called me worthless and a liar the other day, you startled me into realizing I have been living out the lousy image I have of myself.

"Who am I? What am I? I'm not like anybody else. So I lie, I hide."

"But it's easy to understand why you feel that way."

A red Chevrolet pickup zoomed down the hill. The driver must have spotted us way at the top, because that's when he poked his head out the window, and when he got close, he stuck his hand out and flipped us off. "Faggots!" he screamed. The word seemed to hang in the air forever, even after the sound of his engine had faded away.

My eyes followed the truck all the way down the hill to the bend, trying, but failing, to get a license number. I shrugged. What difference did it make? I'd never be able to annihilate every kid who said something bad. I'd best forget about that. Suck it up.

"Don't worry about those guys," Angel said.

I studied her. "I can't believe your courage, what you did this morning."

"Took no courage at all. I didn't have a choice." She pulled at her braid and inspected the hair at the end, where it was wrapped in a rubber band. "Well, yes, there was another choice. We could've moved again." She swished the braid over her shoulder. Looked at me. "Yes, that's why we moved from Florida to Iowa."

"I don't understand," I said.

"Remember, I said I'd told my best friend my story."

"And she squealed on you."

"Last fall, just as school started in Florida, I'd told Ida one night at her house, during a sleepover. Even about my mom's artificial insemination. First time I'd told anyone that."

"You must've been great friends with her."

"We played basketball together, our team's one-two punch. We were going to be pals forever. But when we had a fight over a boy, and it turned out he liked me, she got so mad she told everyone about me. The boy dropped me, what a jerk. I was so humiliated. In school, everyone stared at me. Whispered. I felt like I was starring in a freak show. Like I had two heads." Faint smile. "That's not as bad as a 'worthless, lying fraud,' though."

I stuffed my hands into my jean pockets. "Sorry."

"I quit basketball, wouldn't go to school. My mom felt so guilty. She's the one who suggested we move in order to give me a fresh start. Diane agreed." Angel pushed herself off the Jeep's hood and stood in front of me. "That's my last secret, Danny. Honest." She took a breath. "Except I have one more thing to say."

I braced myself.

"What?"

"I told everyone in class this morning because I finally realized I have to be who I am. I got some excellent basketball genes from someone."

"You're more than a great basketball player. You're a beautiful girl who—"

She put a finger to my lips. "Shhh. I told because, unlike Florida, here I have someone I want to be with."

I reached for her, wanted to hold her, hug her, kiss her.

But Angel held me off, palms pushed into my chest.

"No," she said, "I want you to know you don't have to go through this with me. I can do this on my own. I have to do it, you don't."

"Yes, I do."

"You can't believe what people will say to you because they see you with me, the conclusions they'll jump to, how they'll ignore you. All kinds of things. Stop being your friend. Just terrible stuff."

"I know." I told her about my day, about Kristin, Melody, Tony, Stinocher.

"It'll get worse," Angel said. "You ready for hate mail, telephone calls? You up for that?"

I grabbed her shoulders and said, "You're not going to talk me out of this."

"Do you love me like your note said?"

"I wouldn't have written that if I didn't."

"Say it. I want to hear you say it."

"I love you."

Her lips quivered. "I love you, too."

Then she hobbled down into the grassy ditch alongside the road.

"What are you doing?" I cried. "You'll get poison ivy."

She picked a bouquet of the white flowers from the ditch, scrambled back up, and handed them to me. "Here. For you, Queen Anne's Lace. I love the rose you gave me. When I saw it on the mantel, I cried, but I was still so mad at you."

I set the flowers on the hood of my Jeep and kissed her. I could've kissed her all year.

I heard a car roaring down the hill, horn blaring, but we ignored the sound and kept on kissing. When we stopped, Angel whipped out that progress chart from her back pocket, all marked "excellent," poked a finger at it, and said, "I want to verify this! Immediately. One hundred shots. The closest place is the gym."

"Are you sure?"

"I'm not letting you back out of this, Danny. Let's go."

No point in arguing.

24.

I gathered the flowers off the Jeep's hood, we jumped in, and I drove up to the school parking lot, now practically empty.

We held hands going into the building and down the hallway. Big River High has a No Public Display of Affection policy, which includes holding hands. Kids pretty much ignore it, though, unless a teacher or administrator is in sight.

Angel walked smoothly in her new cast. Almost normal. A few kids were hurrying out of the building and didn't seem to notice Angel and me, but I looked back to see if they were looking back. They were.

Their heads zipped around when they saw me eyeing them.

While Angel waited in the gym, I snatched a basketball from the boys' locker room.

Dad sat in his office at his desk, shuffling through papers, spotted me, and stepped into the doorway. He leaned against the doorjamb, pencil behind his ear.

"What are you doing with the basketball?" he said.

I figured now was not the time to be evasive, so I said, "I'm going to shoot free throws with Angel."

He straightened. "I thought that ended. Didn't she knock you into Duck Creek?"

"We've worked through a couple of problems. Everything's going to be okay. Still want to meet her?"

"What I'd like you to do is think about this again. Come in here."

"She's waiting in the gym, Dad."

"I wish you wouldn't do this."

I bounced the basketball a couple of times.

"Give her up," he said.

He turned away and walked back into his office. I poked my head inside the doorway, but I wasn't going in.

"Is it okay if I bring her home, like, maybe later this afternoon? Or tonight? You said once to bring her around."

I cleared my throat.

I didn't know what he'd say now.

He didn't look at me. He sank into the chair behind his desk. Pulled the chair forward. Shuffled papers again.

"Is tonight okay?" I said.

His gaze was so penetrating I almost looked away.

He gave a tight nod. "Bring her around. Ask her if she likes spaghetti."

I grinned. "All right. I will."

He'd come a long way. I couldn't ask for more than that, though I know he still felt Angel was bad for me. It was up to Angel and me to prove him wrong. If we could.

Angel sat in the bleachers in the gym. A dozen or so guys were playing shirts and skins at one end, five or six girls watching. Two teachers slapped a badminton birdie at each other over a net in a far corner.

I trotted in with the ball. This is where it had all started only two months ago, with hundreds of kids screaming in the bleachers for Angel McPherson as she whipped me. I'd been plenty nervous. I felt a little bit the same way right now because I hadn't practiced a lick recently.

Angel met me under the basket.

I spun the ball on my finger, and said, "You want to know my last and final secret?"

She laughed and said, "Your dad's gay."

I laughed at that, too. "And that reminds me, when we finish here, you're coming over tonight to meet him. Okay?"

She thought a moment. "You want me to?"

"Yes. You like spaghetti?"

"Love it." She held her hand out. "Give me the ball."

I held back. "Not yet," I said. "Now is the time to reveal my secret. I haven't practiced very much—"

"That's no secret."

"—but with about two weeks' work, I'll be able to whip you."

"In your dreams."

"You're not all that good."

I arched a shot from the corner, praying for a break, a miracle. Something. Anything. My shot hit the far rim and bounded away. Angel scooted after it, dribbled out to three-point range, and standing there, off balance on only one good ankle, probably not having touched a basketball in weeks, tossed in a swisher. No sweat, so sweet.

She grinned. "One hundred shots, Danny. Maybe two. Or more. Depends how well you do."

"I'll make a bet," I said. "After two weeks, I'll be able to beat your ass."

"What's the bet?"

"A quarter," I said.

I noticed people in the gym had stopped to watch us.

"All right," she said. "I'll bet a quarter. A quarter you never beat me. Tie me, maybe, because I'm going to make sure you improve, but never beat me."

"Never beat you?"

"Never ever. For a quarter."

"A bet," I said.

"Then let's shake."

She flipped her hand out, flashing her smile.

"I'm the best big mistake you ever made," I said. I grabbed her hand and shook it, while making a deep bow.

Then despite the school's NPDA policy, I kissed her on the lips in the gym for everyone to see. Students. Teachers. That would ignite some hot gossip. Mr. Anderson, one of the faculty badminton players, was already striding toward Angel and me, all red-faced, pounding the edge of his racquet in the palm of his hand. My dad would probably know in thirty seconds.

Did I care?

No.

I'd fallen in love with the girl who was going to teach me how to shoot free throws. What else mattered?

"Cool," she said, and kissed me back.